Kikitu and the Stolen Children Mystery

Best Wishes   Tommy Conner

by

Tommy Conner

Illustrations by
Angela Gooliaff

For
Stephanie
Always

SILVERTON DAILY SENTINAL

RCMP are baffled by missing children. Eight have mysteriously vanished in the last two years. The public are being asked to help. For her knowledge of the terrain and people Yuka, Kikitu and the whole sled dog team will be asked to join the police in the search to find answers to this mystery. The latest victims are from the village of Isachuk. If you have any information call the RCMP non-emergency help line.

CHAPTER ONE

Two police RCMP pick-up trucks, with snowmobiles on the back, were parked outside Grandfather's house as Yuka walked home from school.

It was unusual for one, never mind two police vehicles to be here in a small village so she was intrigued. She wondered if she had done anything wrong but could not think of anything.

As she entered the house, there was a noise from the back room so she made her way there. Her grandfather, Jaekwan, the village elder, was sitting at the kitchen table. Opposite him was a man with black hair in braids (pigtails), next to him was a white man with reddish hair and beard, both in police uniforms.

"Yuka, these men are here to see you."

"Why? What have I done?" she asked.

"Nothing, nothing they just want to talk to you. This is Constable Tim Happ and Sergeant Sam Running Rabbit." They both smiled at her. The sergeant had a bright white smile but the constable's smile only seemed to be a movement of his beard upwards at the sides. "Hi, Yuka. Call me Sam."

"You must be Indigenous with a name like Running Rabbit."

"That's right! Our grandfather would seek a name from spiritual dreams and name us after what he saw in the dream," he said.

"Luckily, he did not see a lame duck," Yuka joked. They all laughed.

"Nice one," the constable said. "Sam Daffy Duck."

"You should talk," the sergeant countered to his companion. "His name is like that of a coffee and doughnut shop that he cannot pass without going in. Right, Timmy?"

"Well, Yuka, what does your name mean?" Sam asked.

"My name means 'Bright Star' so maybe my mother gave birth under the moon and stars."

"Nice, I like that," Sam commented.

Jaekwan interrupted them. "They want you to go to the police detachment and answer some questions about local people and places."

"Why?"

4

"We were told back in Silverton, on our way up here, that you know the wilderness and its people better than anyone around here. We just need your help in an investigation."

"I need to look after the dogs. They get a run every night. Cannot miss it," Yuka asserted.

"I will do it tonight," Grandfather said.

"Kikitu, the lead dog, won't be happy if he does not go with me."

"It's only for a short time. I'll take care of him. Now the quicker you go the quicker you will be back. I have given the key to the sergeant here."

Reluctantly, she led them out the house and they took off towards the town centre, with Yuka directing them.

In remote wilderness districts of Nunavut, some towns only have a small detachment, usually a mobile home type building with a desk or two, phone and computer links, and a couple of jail cells. The village elder usually holds the key.

Entering the station, it was cold and quite dark inside. Yuka turned on the lights while one officer searched to turn up the heat and the other switched on the computer.

The station was one big room with two jail cells separated from the rest of the area by bars. Each cell had a bed and a washbasin next to a toilet, with a little curtain that could be drawn around it.

"Right," Sam started. "I will get right to it. You may know that several children have gone missing. Eight to be exact."

"Eight!" Yuka exclaimed. "That many? I only know a couple around here. That is Osha and Ujurak Auka."

"That is the couple we want to talk to you about. There were six others but not from around here. The Auka boy and girl were just recently filed as missing. So, we were sent to investigate the disappearances."

"How long has this been going on?" Yuka asked.

"About two years."

"Two years! And you are just getting around to it now?" She could feel her face getting flush with anger. Her parents had both been missing for over two years. Normally, on school break she would take a trip to extended family, relatives or friends of theirs, to check if they had any news. She had never given up trying to find them.

"No, no," Sam stated. "We have investigated the others, compiled evidence and conducted searches without success. The strange thing is that there are no clues as to where they went, no DNA or tracks in the snow leading away from the abductions.

"If they were kidnapped, no ransom was ever asked for. If they were snatched, we do not know why. It's been one dead end after another so we are hoping to get lucky here."

"If the ground was covered in snow there had to be tracks," Yuka stated.

"Seems they all went missing in the middle of snowstorms and any tracks got covered in fresh snow or blown away in the wind."

"Do you have a map with each abduction marked out?" she asked.

"Yes." He clicked away at the computer while they all huddled around it. The display screen came up with a map with red dots marked in a horseshoe pattern.

"Whoever did it," Yuka started, "if they planned it during snowstorms, they must have good weather reading skills or weather pattern read-outs from meteorologists or weathermen."

"Possibly," Sam stated. "But what do you make of the pattern of locations?"

She studied the map for a while. "Looks to me like they were centred around a point where they could take the children back to a hideout." Yuka pointed with her hand to the screen. "In the middle there are the Siminuk Mountains and if that is where they are located then it will be almost impossible to find them. You can easily get lost there."

"You ever been there?" Tim asked.

"Once," she replied. "If it were not for the dogs, I don't think I could have found my way out."

"Do you know where the Auka family is living? We need to talk to them and we were hoping you could show us," the sergeant explained.

"They move around a lot, but I think they may be around an inukshuk north of here. It has special spiritual meaning to them. I think one of their ancestors is buried near there."

"Well can you take us there? If they are not at that location then we would have no idea where to go, but you might."

"It is a school break for the Christmas period but I would need Grandfather's permission."

"We already asked him, and he agreed as long as you are back before school starts up. So, will you take us?" Sam asked again.

"How are we going to travel?" she queried "I will only go with the dogs and they will be slower than your snowmobiles."

"That's okay. We'll go at your speed. We need you to guide us so it's not a problem."

"Fine then. Do you want to start first thing tomorrow?" Yuka asked.

"Yes, we'll bunk down in the cells tonight." Tim nodded towards the beds behind the bars. "It won't be the first time or the last, I guess. Is there a café nearby?"

"There is only one. It is located inside the only grocery store in town, a Northmart store two streets west of here," she answered.

"Good enough then. We will see you first thing in the morning. Does it ever get light here?"

"Not at this time of year. You will have to wait another few months for that, but it will get a little lighter about 7:00 a.m. It's called astronomical twilight."

Yuka left them to it and began walking home. She pulled out a dog whistle, long and thin and blew on it. If the dogs were close by, they would come to her no matter what Grandfather said.

Shortly after, they came pounding around a corner, tails wagging, and tongues hanging out.

CHAPTER TWO

First thing in the morning, Yuka started loading the sled. The dogs were all jumping around excitedly. They could tell they were going out on the trail because otherwise it would only be a run in the evening.

She packed her tent, bedding, food, and blankets, then dog bowls, kibble and a bag of frozen raw fish, camping stove and gear, as much as she thought they might need for a few days away.

"You have your satellite phone and GPS transceiver, right?" her grandfather asked.

"Yes, I never go anywhere without them, you know that. The batteries are fully charged."

"Good, so keep in touch and take care."

They said their goodbyes, then the sled dogs took off up the street. It was early, so not many people were around but those that were waved to her, everyone knew everyone else in the small village.

The snowmobiles were loaded and the RCMP officers were finishing off their checks on the machines and making sure extra fuel tanks were loaded on the side. They greeted her as the team of dogs pulled up alongside.

"Morning! We are ready to go if you are," Sam stated.

"I am ready," Yuka replied. "But I thought the Royal Canadian Mounted Police always used horses."

"That was in older times," Tim began. "But snow is hard on our horses so we use the snowmobiles in these conditions. We're faster and more mobile, especially in rugged mountain areas."

"Okay," she replied. "But you will follow me, right? I don't want the dogs breathing your exhaust fumes."

"Lead the way," the sergeant agreed. "We will be right behind you."

"Hike!" Yuka shouted and the dogs took off. It only took a couple of blocks till they were out into the wilderness.

Light snow blew in the wind making the trail hard to see but the dogs always took the easier path, clipping along at a nice steady pace but still quicker than a walk. If Yuka got off the back to guide the sled around a bush or a bump she had to run, then jump back on again. The snowmobiles were in line astern behind her, the officers sitting down comfortably at the slower speed and gazing around at the scenery.

Mountains in the distance grew closer as they journeyed mile after mile, the surroundings quiet except for the occasional yelp from the dogs and the burbling exhaust sound from the snow machines.

They came to a river, slow moving and partially covered in ice. Yuka guided them along the bank towards the only bridge for miles around and stopped before crossing.

"This bridge is old so we will cross it one at a time," she declared. "I'll go first."

"Hike!" she called jumping onto the back of the sled. It was not a long bridge and as Kikitu reached the far end the sled was still at the beginning. After crossing over, Yuka went a little further and stopped, waiting for the others. Just as she turned to look for them there was an almighty crack as the bridge gave way under the weight of two snowmobiles.

"Idiot *Anguns*! Idiot men!" she called out running back to the bridge.

Amongst the wooden bridge wreckage, the first snowmobile was at the bank edge nearest Yuka the other was in the middle of the river. Luckily, it was shallow, and the men were only submerged up to their knees.

"What were you thinking? I told you one at a time!" she shouted at them.

"I thought you said, 'you follow mine.'" Tim called out from the middle of the water. "Or something like that. I misunderstood you."

"Ahh!" Yuka called out in frustration. "Wait there. I'll get the dogs to pull you out."

She ran back to the sled and took out a loop of rope then disconnected the tug line from the sled and urged the dogs to follow her.

Reaching the bank edge, she threw one end of the rope to Sam in the first snowmobile and told him to tie it to the machine then tied off the other end to the dog's tug line.

Standing on the bank so she could see both the dogs and the snow machine, Yuka called out for the dogs to take the strain then called out, "Hike, hike!"

Slowly the machine inched up the bank. Sam steered it as best he could till it crested the top edge of the river bank and the dogs kept pulling it forward till Yuka called "Whoa" for them to stop.

The sergeant untied the rope from the machine and Yuka took it from him.

"You better see if it will start again while I get your partner."

Returning to the bank, she threw the rope to Tim who attached it to the machine. She could hear the other machine cranking over and finally start up.

"I can pull it out with this machine," he called out.

"*Too late!* This one is nearly out," Yuka shouted back above the sound of the snowmobile revving up.

Easily cresting the riverbank, the dogs pulled the machine a little further on and stopped.

"See if you can restart the machine," she said taking the rope from the constable.

As she hooked the dogs back up to the sled and stowed the rope away, the second machine burst into life and revved up with a little smoke coming out the back.

Gathering the men together she asked, "How wet are you? Are you soaked to the skin?"

"Yes," Tim replied. "Well, my feet are."

"Me too," Sam added.

20

"We are about an hour away from the inuksuk. We either get there fast as we can or we make a fire here and dry your clothes off. We do not want your feet getting frostbite. They could turn black. Then you would have to have your toes removed."

Alarm showed in their eyes at the thought of losing their toes. "We better make a fire here," they both agreed as their survival training knowledge kicked in.

"Right, we will have to use some camp stove fuel to get a fire going. I will get it started," she looked around and spotted a clump of bushes and short scrub trees. "Go gather some kindling and what-ever else will burn."

Yuka grabbed the camp stove fuel and set to work. "Okay, take your boots off and stick them in front of the fire," Yuka ordered as the men returned with a couple of armloads of firewood.

Soon they were huddled around the glowing fire, the men sitting on some stones with their feet towards the fire. Yuka fed the dogs then came back to them.

"Have you not done wilderness survival training?" she asked.

"Yes," they both replied.

"Then you both should know better than to take chances. It is easy to get into trouble out here; a wrong move, and you could die. If you are not sure what we are doing then ask."

They both looked sheepish and did not reply.

"You are lucky there are a few bushes clinging to the soil around here. The official tree line is south of the village but it is not a clear-cut line, trees still pop up where they can. I am going to call Grandfather to tell him about the bridge, warn others who may want to use it, and organise repairs."

"Tell him we are sorry," Sergeant Sam replied.

Yuka pulled out her satellite phone turned the antenna and punched in the numbers. "Grandfather, what have you gotten me into? The police just broke the Laddu Bridge and now it will need repairs. We are getting them dried out now after they fell into the water."

They spoke for a few minutes as she explained the situation, her grandfather making excuses for the RCMP, telling her they were not as experienced as she was about the dangers out there.

CHAPTER THREE

"*Should we camp here for the night or* carry on?" Yuka asked. "If we continue and cannot find the Auka family we will have to use our own fuel or we can use it now and set up camp here."

The two police officers looked at each other before the sergeant spoke. "We should carry on and try to find the family. We're okay if you are. We need to get some answers before the trail goes cold."

"Right. Let's go then. I will put out the fire while you make sure your machines are all right."

Yuka jumped up, grabbed the camp stove and packed everything on the sled then damped down the fire with snow. She picked up the extra branches that had been gathered and stowed them on the sled tied down with some rope.

"Good firewood is hard to find out here so we take it with us if we can. You never know when you might need it. You cannot waste resources out here," she called out as the men watched.

The men had the snowmobiles running so Yuka urged the dogs forward and took the lead. They soon reached their normal cruising speed of a long loping stride that covered distance fast. She stared ahead and thought she could see the tall outline of an inuksuk in the distance.

Dark black stone arms pointing outwards as directions to lost or weary travellers seeking refuge in a vast wilderness of snow and mountains. The longest arm always pointed towards the nearest settlement, which was back the way they came at Isachuk.

Long before they got there, she could see a couple, man and a woman, standing watching them approach. In a land of very few people newcomers were studied from afar to check if they knew who they were or even if they might be a threat.

Getting closer, the couple waved their arms when they recognised Yuka and the sled dog team. She headed directly to them and pulled up alongside. Only the man had his head exposed and the woman's head was covered by the large hood of her *amauti*, the parka worn by Inuit women.

"*Yuka, ih-hi*, nice to see you again," the woman greeted her.

"*Ih-hi*, I have brought the RCMP to speak with you," she said greeting her back. "They are Sergeant Sam Running Rabbit and Constable Tim Happ."

They came forward and were given a hug by the couple as Yuka introduced them. "This is Aga, the children's mother and Toklo, their father."

The man stepped forward, his long straggly grey hair blowing in the breeze away from his brown weather-beaten skin, a few stubbles of hair sprouting from his chin by way of a beard.

"*Unnukkut*," he said. The two officers looked at Yuka.

"It means evening or good evening." They nodded back at the man who beckoned them towards their home, which was a dug-out in a snowbank.

A short tunnel-like entrance gave way to a single circular room, ice blocks were stacked like a wall, the roof was a dome-like structure and in the middle a metal smoke stack protruded to the outside. Standing in the middle of the room was a square stove for burning wood or any other flammable material that was readily available.

The residents quickly removed their parkas and the officers did the same as the heat inside was very pleasant. Yuka kept her coat on.

"If you are going to talk for a while I will see to the dogs. I guess we are staying here the night?"

Sam nodded and Yuka left.

Once outside, she moved the sled to alongside the Auka's snowmobile then started unhitching the dogs and stowing the harness onboard the sled ready for the next day. As she was about to feed them, she had a thought and went back inside.

They looked up as she entered. "Do you have some of the children's clothes here?"

"Yes," Aga replied then stood up, went to a corner and pulled out some clothes, undergarments mostly because people did not go outside without wearing parkas. She handed them to her.

They all looked at her curiously as she left. Yuka turned to them. "Just a thought."

Outside, she gathered the dogs to her, all roaming loose, and dumped the clothes on the ground.

"Find. Find." She called pointing to the clothes. Some she held to their noses, some she just let sniff.

"Find!" she called out again.

Seemingly running around in circles, the dogs all had their noses to the ground sniffing here there and everywhere. It looked like a waste of time till one by one each came to be turning towards the mountains and started to walk that way.

Yuka called the group outside and without outer clothes they stood up as Yuka pointed towards the dogs leaving.

"I asked them to 'Find,' pointing at the clothes. "And they all want to go that way. I think the children are in that direction."

"You think they may have picked up their scent?" Toklo asked.

"Possibly. It may be faint but gives us a direction to go look," Yuka replied.

She pulled out her dog whistle and blew. It made no sound to the human ear but the dogs turned around and sprinted back towards her.

"I am going to feed them now and settle them to make snow beds then I will be coming inside."

One by one the adults retreated inside the lodge.

Yuka petted each dog in turn as reward for their work.

After feeding them, then settling down the dogs for the night she picked up the clothes and returned inside and gave the clothes back to Aga. Pulling off her parka they gave her some food that had been saved, and she began eating what was left of a stewed rabbit.

"Do you think we can use the dogs to start a search for the children?" Sam asked.

"Yes, if you want. But I am not sure where it will take us or even if the dogs are on the right scent," she replied.

"We have gone over every detail of their abduction with Toklo and Aga without discovering anything new. Just like the others in the middle of a storm they disappeared. It seems they were all asleep and somehow the children got up, dressed then went outside never to be seen again."

Aga had tears in her eyes. "We searched every-where, all the usual places where we hunt, fish or where the kids played . . . nothing."

"Don't worry," Tim said. "We will do our best to find them, our bosses said not to come back without answers, and with our top guide," he indicated Yuka. "We will find out what happened."

"Humph," Yuka murmured at the mention of her name then turned to Sam. "Do you have any guns if we get into trouble?"

"Glad you mentioned that," he jumped up. "I want to show you something." Sam left the lodge and returned minutes later carrying a rifle in a special bag. Opening it up, he showed them the weapon and drew out a small case.

"This is a dart gun and these are drug darts." He displayed them to everyone. "Our science team back at headquarters issued this to us with instructions on how to use them. If we come across any unusual animals, they want us to get DNA and tissue samples."

"What sort of animals?" Yuka asked.

"There have been some reports of polar bears and grizzly bears coming in contact, fighting over food, things like that and they may have interbred, you know polar bear fathers and grizzly mothers. They call them Grizlars but that might just be made up tales. Have you seen anything like that?" Sam looked at the Inuit adults and Yuka.

"Never even heard of that," Toklo stated. "We get occasional grizzly bears in the summer but no polar bears this far inland."

"Sounds like a made-up story to me," Yuka agreed.

"Well, just to let you know we do have weapons so you don't have to worry," Sam assured them.

There were furs laid out around the room and Aga pointed out one for Yuka to sleep on. Slightly smaller than the rest it was meant for a child. Blankets were handed out so everyone settled down for the night. The RCMP men took a stroll outside first, probably wanting to talk things over.

CHAPTER FOUR

Early the next morning, Yuka was first up, slipped on her parka and mukluks and then went outside. Her priority job every morning was to feed, water, and check the dogs over making sure none were ill or limping or showing any signs of distress.

After that she cleaned herself up, took off her clothes and rubbed herself clean with snow. It was a ritual in the wilderness. There was no running water unless a stream was nearby. She was used to the cold but when she got home after a trip, she loved to have a shower and shampoo her hair.

When she got dressed again, she went back in the lodge. She found Aga cooking food on the stove. Toklo had gone outside to get clean and the RCMP were stirring, trying to wake up and get going.

Breakfast was herbal tea, bannock bread wrapped around sticks and cooked on top of the stove till golden brown. Aga had also made some *suaasat* for their flasks to take on the journey. The officers had never tried the bannock bread but really enjoyed it.

When he came back, Toklo looked at the other men and spoke. "I would like to come with you, but I need to see to my supplies and hunting lines for food. I also need fuel for the snowmobile."

"If you are going to town you need to know the Laddu Bridge is broken." Yuka told him. "You will have to go the long way around. I did let Grandfather know but the repairs won't be done yet."

"That was our fault," Tim admitted. "Sorry."

"It was old anyway," Toklo replied. "It needed to be replaced."

They all chatted around breakfast, about their lives up till now and how they got to this point, then preparations for the journey began. Yuka hitched up the dogs then packed up the sled. The men put some more fuel from jerry cans into the snowmobiles and stowed away all their stuff.

It was a bright morning, the mountains in the distance bathed in the dim light of the day and surrounded by blue sky, they looked really close as if you could just reach out and touch them.

Aga and Toklo stood by as they were ready to depart, Yuka asked for some children's clothes again, and she went around holding the clothes to each dog's nose then stuck them in the sled before giving the command.

"Find! Hike!" They took off like a rocket, full of energy and willingness to get on with the task at hand. As the snowmobiles passed, they all waved goodbye, everyone hoping to find the children.

The Inuit couple gazed after them and stood watching till they were out of sight heading towards the mountains, the dogs leading the way, making the occasional yelp.

Kikitu turned his head towards Sitka the younger of the lead dogs.

"These human pups we are trying to find must be very important to send the two male humans out in machines. We could probably find them on our own."

"Maybe they thought Yuka could not do it all by herself, or needs protection, they have got guns," he replied.

Turning his head towards the back. "*Can you all still detect the scent of the young pups?*"

"*I can't,*" Zaria answered.

"*Neither can I,*" Taeko agreed.

"*What about the rest of you?*" Kiki asked.

"*Very faint,*" Neo and Fluff stated from near the back.

"*How about you? Blazer, you are good at tracking.*"

"*It is hard to tell which direction, but I think we are going the right way.*"

Granite agreed with him.

"*Sure, it is faint to me as well, but I am sure we are on the right track.*"

They kept their heads low and their noses close to the ground as they pushed on. Mile after mile the mountains got closer till the dogs came to a stop.

"To the right," Kikitu said.

"No, to the left," Sitka argued.

The others were just as divided – some to the left some to the right.

Yuka jumped off the back of the sled then walked to the front, the snowmobiles behind stopped and waited.

"What's going on?" she questioned as the front two were jumping in different directions. "Does the trail split here?"

"What's up?" Sam shouted.

"They seem to be unsure which is the right direction. Can you come up here?"

The engines were switched off and both men walked up to Yuka.

"Let's take a break. There seems to be a split in the trail." She started unhooking the two lead dogs. "I am going to follow Kikitu. See where the trail leads, if one of you will follow Sitka."

Sam agreed to go with Sitka and put his hand on top of the harness. They turned off to the left.

Welcoming a break, the other dogs lay down in the snow to cool off as Kikitu and Yuka walked away to the right, Sam and Sitka to the left till both dogs and humans disappeared from sight.

Nose to the ground Kikitu only traversed a short distance when he stopped. It was a dead end. They turned around and went back. Same thing with Sitka, they got back to find Yuka returning and walking up to the group.

"Dead end," she announced.

"Same here," Sam verified.

"I think—" Yuka started, "that the children tried to escape here, one going one way the other in the opposite direction but were recaptured. I suggest giving the dogs another chance to go straight."

"You could be right," Sam agreed. "Let's carry on."

"Hike!" Yuka shouted as she jumped onto the back of the sled.

The dogs soon got up to speed, their tongues hanging out of open mouths as usual. Once again Kikitu turned to Sitka.

"Did you smell something funny back there?"

"Yes," he replied. *"But I could not tell what it was, not human and no animal I had ever smelled before."*

"Me too. It was certainly not human, but what could it be?"

With no answers they stuck their heads down and got up to a flying trot pace.

Late in the afternoon the sky grew even darker with threatening black clouds appearing with rapid movements across the mountains, Yuka called a halt.

"Looks like a storm is coming," she called to the men. "We better find a good sheltered spot to camp for the night."

The men held their thumbs up in agreement and Yuka carried on.

Low hills were giving way to the start of the mountain range and the convoy skirted around them till she spotted a small bluff or steep bank, beside a ravine or plain. It had a walled cliff with a broad face. She guided the dogs to pull alongside.

"This should do here," she stated to the men. "If you back up your machines to the wall you can pitch the tents between them. It will give you more shelter. I will set up next to you along the cliff face, and the dogs will shelter between all of us."

The men did not argue with her at all, not after the bridge episode, so they set about building tents, unhitching and feeding the dogs and having an evening meal over the camp stove. It was too windy to build a campfire, also there was not enough wood.

After eating they all settled into their tents for the night, with the dogs surrounding Yuka's tent.

CHAPTER FIVE

A howling wind made it difficult to sleep, the gusts blowing the tent cover first one way then another making a flapping noise almost enough to make it snap or tear, but it held, though not enough to make sleep possible.

Yuka dozed in and out of sleep not able to do much more than listen to the wind till the dogs started barking, loudly and urgently. Something was bothering them. They were aggressively fighting, or so it seemed.

She pulled the zipper to open the flap of the tent and stuck her head outside. A white-out made it impossible to see anything. Snow was falling hard and fast, blowing into her face. The barking directed her to look to the right but she could not see a single thing except a white blanket in front of her.

Normally, the dogs were close by but she could not see any of them. She just heard barking, growling and snapping as swirling masses of snowsqualls flashed across her eyes. She pulled her head back inside to put on her parka and mukluks before pulling the tent zipper fully open and stepping out.

Working along the bluff wall towards the noise of the barking she still could not see anything just feel her way in the blizzard. Then the barking stopped. The dogs turned up at her side one by one.

Whatever was bothering them seemed to have gone so she thought it best to return to her tent and wait out the storm then try and find out what happened later.

Her sleeping bag was still a little warm as she snuggled back inside, most of the dogs wanted to get into the tent with her but there was not enough room so she shooed them all out and pulled the zipper back down. She always felt bad leaving them out in a storm but they were used to it and huddled together to keep warm.

It was almost morning when the wind died down, the tent flapping stopped and went quiet Thankful for the peaceful silence she fell asleep. It went past her normal time to get up when she was woken up by the dogs, not barking but restless, treading around waiting to be fed.

Rising up, she slipped on her parka and mukluks opened up the tent then stretched her body and legs outside. The sky was a dark bright blue, the weather calm as she went to her sled for dog food. They devoured the frozen fish and kibble with relish, wagging their tails and sniffing around for leftovers.

As she finished feeding them, she noticed it was very quiet, with no sound from the men, so she strolled over to their tents. The first one was empty, the second one also. She stared around, perhaps they had gone to clean up, out of sight for modesty, but there was no sign of them. It was worrying so she walked nearby close to the campsite – still no sign of them.

She lit her camp stove to make some *suaasat* for breakfast, thinking they would turn up in a moment. Maybe they went to survey the land for possible routes.

By the time the food was warm they still did not appear so she ate alone, all the time looking and listening for the two men to appear or turn up, but nothing.

Yuka walked back to the tents then noticed something strange. There were no footprints

She knew the storm would have covered up the tracks in the night but surely they would not have left in the middle of a blizzard.

Some of the dogs were finished eating and were wandering around with her as she paced up and down, finally coming to a conclusion. She was all alone. The men had been taken, by whom she could not tell but there was no other answer.

The barking in the middle of the night must have been when it happened and the dogs brawling was them protecting her from whatever it was. It was a mystery. She had no answers and sat on the edge of the sled wondering what to do next.

Kikitu sat beside her. Then the others came over and sat or lay down in front of her. She then began talking to them knowing full well that they did not understand a word but it helped her think things through.

"If I phone Grandad, I know he will tell me to come home, that the RCMP will send more officers to find them or search for them. That may be too late though. The trail will be cold." Yuka then thought about her special friend who she had actually rescued on a previous adventure. "If I phone the North Pole what would Santa tell me to do? He might send Skoop or some elves but that will take time as well."

She sat still for a while, the dogs turning their heads from side to side pondering what she was doing, till she seemed to make up her mind.

"We will follow them. You know how to find them, right? But the men will not be able to return or travel without a snowmobile, so I will tie our sled behind a machine and let you all travel untethered, sniffing a trail while I follow in a snowmobile pulling our sled behind."

Her mind made up she began preparations, packing her sled first, putting the tent onboard, setting all the dog harness inside and tying it all down securely. Going over to the snowmobiles she checked them and noticed one had the dart gun fixed to the side but no other weapons. She made sure the fuel was topped up then started it up and pulled up in front of her sled.

Securing the tug line to the back of the snowmobile she was ready to go but first she took the dogs to the tents and had them sniff all around, then jumping back on the snow machine she shouted to them.

"Find! Find! *Hike!*"

Kikitu seemed to understand and took off running up an unseen trail with only scent guiding him. The others quickly joined him; Sitka next to the lead dog then others teaming up as if they were pulling a sled. Yuka smiled at the idea that they formed a team even though they were not tethered together. The snowmobile easily kept up as she let them lead the way.

"What was that thing last night?" Kikitu asked Sitka. *"It was so big and hairy."*

"Don't know," he replied. *"But the smell, it was the same as we noticed before and the strange noise it made."*

"I know, never heard anything like it, a humming low noise. What was that? It made me feel weak, like slowing me down. Did you feel the same?"

"I did," Blazer said from behind them. *"Me too, and me."* They all seemed to agree.

"Well, one thing," Kikitu stated. *"The trail is easy to follow and we are not far behind. We will easily catch them."*

The ground got steeper as they climbed into the mountains, everywhere the scenery changed the higher they rose up. The snow got deeper, making it harder for the dogs but the snowmobile was fine as long as it kept moving, Yuka knew if she stopped it would sink and be difficult to get going again.

She noticed a pouch mounted inside the machine and found it held a pair of binoculars. On a flat surface she would stand up and scan the landscape, searching for any sign of movement or marks that may show a trail.

Kikitu and the team slowed down as the slope got steeper and their legs weaker from having to jump or pull out of deeper and deeper snow. Yuka was unsure whether or not to turn around and go back

but saw they were nearly at the top of an embank-
ment so she spun past the dogs and made an
easier path for them with the snowmobile plowing
a corridor.

Reaching the top, she could see they were on a
plateau or flat plain and the snow was firmer.
Stopping, she waited for the dogs and scanned
the landscape again. She thought there was movement far off in the distance and tried to zoom in
but was not sure. Whatever it was blended into
the whiteness.

Panting, the dogs crested the rise and flopped down
beside her. Luckily, they did not have to pull the
sled or they would have been too exhausted and
unable to go on. She let them rest and roll in the
snow to cool down.

When she thought they had rested enough Kikitu
was roused and padded off, the others followed in

the direction she had guessed there was movement while the snowmobile crept along behind them.

They were slower than before but kept up a good pace. Within an hour they were at the spot where Yuka was sure she had seen movement. Skirting around a tall grey rock another flat plain was before them. This time she glimpsed movement ahead and pulled out the binoculars.

Focusing on the spot she could not see anything. Either she was not looking at the right spot or it had dropped out of sight. She urged the dogs on with a feeling they were closing in on their quarry or target. The pack ran faster and faster till they reached the end and the trail dropped down. They stopped dead in their tracks. Yuka stopped the machine and ran over to look at what had halted them.

CHAPTER SIX

The edge of the plain dropped down to a large ledge about one hundred feet below. Yuka looked over the ridge then ran back to grab the binoculars. She could not believe what she saw!

Coming back to the edge she dropped flat on her belly to peer over. The dogs all copied her. Only their heads peeped over as she brought the binoculars up to her eyes and brought the view into focus.

A large campsite was set up with a cavern over to one side. Children were wandering around and the two policemen were lying on a stone table and looked to be either asleep or unconscious.

Yuka started counting, two boys together another three girls moving logs. Around them by the cavern's entrance was a girl and two boys, eight! All eight of the missing children were there! She even recognised the two Auka youngsters.

But how had they got there? She did not have to wait long when her heart jumped and pounded as two more adults exited the cavern being pushed along by a huge tall being covered in long white hair. It stood on two legs and walked like a human but certainly was not a human. It was a *Mahaha!*

At first, she took no notice of the adults. Her eyes were glued to the snow being. Her grandfather had told stories about them but they were thought to have died out. He said some had named them as the Canadian cousin to the Yeti (whoever they were) and were stealers of children. From the way he had described them there was no doubt in her mind, this was a *Mahaha*. Grandfather said they stole children and tickled them to death or just abandoned them in the middle of the wilderness.

Her gaze drifted down to the two adults in front and her pounding heart took another huge leap. It was her mother and father being pushed along by the snow being.

"Kiki! It's Mom and Dad!" Keeping the binoculars to her eyes she stretched out a hand and grabbed Kikitu by the fur around his neck.

"It's Mom and Dad! Can you believe it? Two years I have been searching for them, now at last here they are! Kiki, we have to rescue them."

She lay there in the snow examining the area, looking for answers. How deep was the cavern? Were there any more entrances? Where could they surprise the *Mahaha* or get close? A plan began to emerge in her mind.

Yuka rose up and walked back to the snowmobile. She pulled the dart gun out and also a small case holding the drug darts then began examining how to load and fire the weapon. She had never seen a gun like this before. As a child of hunters all Inuit children learned how to safely use a weapon. Even though she could not own a gun till she was twelve and old enough to get a licence, you never knew when you may be attacked or get a chance to find food.

Before she loaded it, she had to become familiar with how to load it, aim it and fire it, all unusual.

A couple of times she lifted it to her shoulder, aimed, and squeezed the trigger. When Yuka thought she could handle it she opened the small case to find two loaded darts inside. Finding where to load one she inserted it into the rifle and stuck the other, inside the case, into her pocket.

Unhitching the sled from the snowmobile she turned to the dogs. "I want all of you to guard the sled while Kiki and I go around and get into the camp from the other side."

Their heads moved side to side and up at her trying to understand. Yuka knew that so just told them to "Stay" and Kiki walked with her back to the snowmobile and drove off, the dog's eyes following them.

At a slow speed to keep the noise down they traversed the ridge about a half-mile till they found another trail going down. She turned the machine down that track with Kikitu following.

Braking to keep the speed down she reached the bottom and turned towards the campsite making as little noise as possible. When they were within sight of the camp a strange noise hit them.

Giggling, loud and clear! Giggling from children and adults. Yuka stopped the machine and dismounted, pulled out the rifle and started creeping forward, staying out of sight and making no noise. Kiki was crouched low.

When they could get a good view the spectacle that greeted them made them stop. Children were lying on the ground, their arms around their chest laughing and giggling as hard as they could, others were sitting up, bent over and holding their ribs.

The *Mahaha* seemed to be smiling as it went around tickling one after another, if one seemed to stop it would go up to them and put both hands around them and take delight in getting them laughing again.

Dog and girl crept forward till suddenly Yuka stopped, stood up and dropped the rifle. A humming noise surrounded them, making Kiki feel weak and putting Yuka into a trance. She took off walking slowly towards the *Mahaha*, summoned by a strange calling she could hear in the humming noise.

Kikitu knew he had to stop her and bit into her coat-tails, pulling her back, but she dragged him along with an unknown strength. He let go, went in front of her and tried to trip her up, but she sidestepped him.

Going in front of her a short way he turned and ran at her then jumped at her chest bowling her over. Her head hit the snow with a thud bringing a cloud of snowflakes around her. She flipped open her eyes, wondering where she was or what was happening. Kiki bit into her parka hood and started dragging her back.

As her senses and memory returned, she turned onto her knees and started crawling away. Grabbing the rifle from where she had dropped it, they ran back to the snowmobile.

"Good boy, thanks Kiki." She petted him around his neck. "That is how it managed to steal the children. I think it is called hypnotism or a sound trance or something like that."

63

She searched around the machine. Coming across a compartment close to where the rifle was, she flipped open the lid and found what she was looking for.

"Ear defenders these are called," she said showing them to the dog. "Used to stop loud noises when you fire a rifle close to your ear. They look like headphones but there are no speakers inside only sound dampening cloth."

Slipping them over her head and ears she then grabbed the rifle. "Let's go."

Shuffling along on their bellies, they got closer and closer. All the humans were in a trance so did not bother or notice them. The *Mahaha* seemed intent on tickling them and was lost in a world of its own.

When she thought she was close enough to get a good shot Yuka lay flat, brought the gun up to her shoulder, steadied herself on her elbows and took aim. They were so close she felt she could not miss, aimed at the torso or biggest part of the being and squeezed the trigger.

Crack! The noise of the gunshot rang around the campsite and the *Mahaha* lifted its head looking for the source of the noise not realizing it had been hit right in the middle of its belly.

It stood upright, its head turning to find the noise then spotted Yuka and Kikitu lying in the snow. Yuka was surprised that the being had not fallen then realised the drug took time to work. She loaded the last dart into the rifle as quick as she could. The *Mahaha* was coming at them.

A little anxious, she pulled the rifle to her shoulder and tried to aim. It was now moving faster towards them. Kikitu jumped up and ran towards it to fend it off, took a leap towards the being when . . . *crack!* The rifle fired again.

Yuka had closed her eyes, hoping she had hit the *Mahaha.* As she looked towards them there was another quieter breaking sound as the ground dropped away under the white snow creature and Kikitu. They disappeared, sinking out of sight in the slipping, sliding movement of snow that was an avalanche.

"No! No! *No!*" Yuka called out as she jumped up and ran towards the edge that was left when the ground sunk down. She gaped at the sight of clouds of snow, huge snowballs and packs of snow thundering down the mountainside. There was no sign of Kiki.

Stunned, she was rooted to the spot unable to grasp the thought that her dog, her best friend, her bonded partner was gone. Time passed till she shook herself. She ran back to the snowmobile.

She had to find him!

CHAPTER SEVEN

Yuka hopped on board the snowmobile, fired it up and began moving towards the edge when Sam came running up.

"Stop!" he shouted. "Stop, it's too dangerous to go down there."

She paid no attention. Nothing was going to prevent her from getting to Kikitu and saving him.

The RCMP officer ran straight at her then jumped onto the back seat.

It was too late to stop her as the snow machine went over the edge. "Zig-zag," he called in her ear. "Slow down, or we will tumble end over end."

She had ridden lots of snowmobiles before but not on a mountainside so she listened to his instructions as they weaved side to side leaning to the uphill side as they made turns. If their speed increased too much Sam called for her to turn upwards to slow them down and keep making turns and weave their way down slowly but safely.

It seemed like forever to Yuka, to get to a lower more level surface created by the avalanche. Then they began looking for either the dog or the *Mahaha*, travelling across the smooth, flat, even plane of snow that had been created.

She felt a sense of panic rise within her as there was no sign of any living being anywhere to be seen. They kept looking as slowly they were getting to the bottom when Sam called out.

"Over there!" He pointed to a darker spot in the snow.

She whipped the throttle open and sped over to the spot, got close, stopped the machine, and jumped off.

It was Kikitu's torn ear sticking out of the snow, quickly they began digging him out, uncovering his head first.

"He's breathing!" Yuka called out as her hopes rose, his nose flaring in and out.

Uncovering the rest of his body, both the humans eased him onto level ground. Yuka began brushing snow off him. He raised his head to lick her when her face was close to his then tried to get up.

The dog could only move on its front legs. Sam eased him down again and looked directly into her eyes.

"He is done for," the sergeant said quietly.

"What do you mean?" Yuka's expression changed to worry.

"His back is broken. He cannot move his back legs."

"No! It cannot be!" she replied as tears formed in her eyes.

"I am sorry. Yuka, but it is true, he is fading away and is probably in a lot of pain." Slowly he pulled out his gun from the side holster.

Tears were rolling down her face till she saw the gun, then she became angry.

"We should put him out of his pain and misery," Sam spoke softly.

"No! *No!* There is *no way* you are going to shoot my dog," Yuka shouted at him.

"It's for the best, Yuka. He will not last long like this. It will be quick. He will never feel a thing. You can walk away and not look." He brought the gun around to point it at Kikitu.

She jumped in front of him. "You are *not* going to kill my dog. I won't allow it! I will tend to him. Put your gun away. He just saved your life and now you want to put him down? *It is not going to happen!* she screamed.

He slowly put the gun back in its holster and thought things over. "Okay, Yuka, have it your way. You are correct. I have no right to put him down."

She cradled Kikitu's head in her arms. "It will be okay, Kiki, I will look after you."

Sam crouched down beside her. "Tell you what, I will go back up top. It's getting even darker, what do you say? I will make sure everyone is okay and try to summon help."

"The rest of the dogs are on the ridge above the campsite along with my sled. Your other snowmobile is back where we camped."

"All right," the sergeant said. "I will leave you alone with Kikitu to nurse him. Maybe in the morning you will change your mind and stop his suffering."

"I won't," she replied defiantly. "Just go and leave us alone. I want to be left alone with him."

Reluctantly Sam got up, mounted the snow machine and sped off up the mountainside.

As soon as he had disappeared, Yuka pulled out her satellite phone, flipped up the antenna and hit the speed dial number one, then listened.

"Yuka? Ho, ho is that you?" Santa answered eventually.

She could not speak as tears rolled down her face, and she sobbed uncontrollably.

"What's up?" he asked. "What's the matter?"

"It's Kikitu!" she blubbered out. "Santa, he is dying."

"How? What happened?"

She blurted out the story in between her sobs.

It was quiet for a moment after she finished, then he spoke. "Yuka do you have your GPS transceiver with you?"

"Yes."

"Then give me your coordinates. I am coming over."

With hopes raised she pulled out the GPS and read out her position to him.

"It will take a little time to hitch up the sleigh, but I will be there as soon as I can."

They both switched off. "You hear that, Kiki? Santa is coming!"

She felt a little better as she looked up to the sky as if willing him to be here right now. Instead, the northern lights came out as if on cue. Bright colours danced across the sky and reflected on the mountains surrounding the young girl embracing the dog in her arms. It felt like they were all alone in the wilderness.

The Auroral display appeared in many colours mostly pale green and pink, but shades of red, yellow, green, blue, and violet could be seen as well. The lights appeared in many forms from patches or scattered clouds of light to streamers, arcs, rippling curtains or shooting rays that lit up the sky with an eerie glow.

She wiped the tears from her cheeks. To her, it would have been the most beautiful place on earth if it were not for the fading animal in her arms. She willed Kikitu to get better while gently stroking him.

Gazing at the sky all the time she anxiously waited. It seemed like forever till she heard a swishing noise, no lights, no bells ringing just a whoosh as he passed over, spotted her, swung around and landed close by.

Still cradling Kiki in her arms, she watched as Santa got out of the sleigh. Mrs. Clause, Jessica, got out the other side and two elves holding bags got out the rear. They approached her and knelt beside her.

"I am sorry, Yuka. Let me talk to Kikitu." Santa gently took the dog's head in his hands.

Jessica lifted Yuka to her feet and hugged her. "We have never met but I feel like I have known you forever. Santa is always telling the story of meeting you and Kikitu getting him home."

"I don't want him to die." She sobbed into Jessica's embrace all the while watching as Santa spoke quietly and the elves placed hands along the dog's back.

Turning to Yuka he said. "We have found where it's broken. We need to operate, now. These are my elf vets who look after the reindeer. We will need to put Kiki under. Understand?"

"Yes," she replied. "Whatever you need to do. Can I help? I want to be a vet after school."

One of the elves took a stethoscope out of a bag. "Hold his head and monitor his breathing and pulse." He placed the scope on Kiki's neck then handed it to her. "If the pulse drops or his breathing seems slow, let us know."

She knelt down, took over from Santa and listened to the stethoscope after moving it around.

CHAPTER EIGHT

An injection by the elves put Kiki to sleep and he went limp in Yuka's arms. Next, the elves placed headlamps over their heads, switched them on to illuminate the operation and began laying instruments beside the dog.

79

Fascinated, she watched as they first opened up the skin across the back, then peeled it back exposing the bone. Even Yuka could see it was bent out of shape but not broken in two. They pulled a small drill out of a bag and one elf placed a clamp over the bones to hold it in the correct position while the other drilled a hole through one bone then another alongside, placed a small plate across the two, and inserted some screws.

Doing this on the other side they then did the same on a lower set of bones correcting the alignment of the backbone spine. Their gloved hands were covered in blood as they cleaned everything up. Resetting the skin covering in place Yuka watched carefully as they stitched it all together till it looked like it had never been apart.

Yuka had watched her mother sew skins together to make the clothes that kept them warm, but she had never seen anything that matched the needlework of the elves.

"We cannot say if Kikitu will ever walk again, but he will live," one of the elves pronounced.

Her eyes started to leak again at the news, floods of tears running down her cheeks. Santa put an arm around her.

"Give it a chance to heal. You never know, he could make a full recovery and if not, you can always make him a small buggy to support his hind legs, and he will be able to run around."

"Why does this happen?" Yuka began. "One moment was pure joy as I found my mother and father, the next was complete misery when Kiki fell down the mountainside."

"This is life, Yuka. The creator of life does not have any favourites or grant happiness when asked. Everyone is treated equally and you have to take the bad as well as the good. Change happens every day and how you cope determines your life. Fate, destiny, and chance are all out of our hands. You must get over the sad times and enjoy the good times."

"But it is so unfair!" she countered.

"I know, I know," he replied trying to comfort her as Jessica also hugged her.

"Now, we must get back before the others come down," Santa stated. "We don't want the rest of the world to know about me."

"But why?" Yuka asked. "Why not let everyone know you are here?"

"It's best people not know," he began. "For one thing people would be flooding onto Christmas Island and stopping our work. Another is that some people believe in me and some people don't. "I think it is up to each person to have a little magic in their lives. It's up to them to choose.

"Older people who still want to believe give each other presents and even add more to their children's gifts because they love them. Most people never want to forget the magical times they had as a child."

Yuka watched as they all clambered into the sleigh, Jessica making sure everyone had their seatbelt fastened, she was kind of particular about safety. Then with a call out to Rudolph, the reindeer galloped forward then leaped into the air. They all waved to Yuka before disappearing into the night sky.

Time had passed so quickly that Yuka had not realised morning was here. She had not slept a wink but that did not matter, she was wide awake and full of energy. She felt full of hope for Kiki and full of hope for a new life back with her mother and father.

Patiently, she waited while watching over Kikitu who was sleeping, breathing steadily, and feeling for a pulse that seemed normal.

When the twilight chased away most of the shadows on the mountain the sound of a snowmobile could be heard high up but getting closer as it weaved its way down towards her. As it came into sight, she could see it was Sam and her sled was being dragged behind. He was all alone and drew the snow machine close and stopped.

"You okay?" he asked. "How is the dog?"

"We are both okay. Kiki is asleep and relaxed," she replied. "He is going to be all right after his bones mend then recovery, healing, and therapy."

Sam knelt down to check out the animal. "I can't believe it! He seems quite normal. What a change from last night! I think you're right. It looks like he will survive." He scratched his head and pulled at his braids as he tried to understand how this remarkable turnaround had happened.

With a shrug of his shoulders he stood up, hesitated while thinking, and then spoke. "I was going to take you and Kiki back up to the ledge and cavern, but

I think maybe we should get them down here." He looked around at the location.

"Why?" she asked.

"I got hold of Divisional headquarters on the sat phone last night and they're sending a team of scientists here by helicopter and to airlift everyone out. The team wants to set up a camp so they can uncover the *Mahaha* and examine it."

Yuka looked at him for more explanation.

"You have done well! I mean all of us. We have recovered the children and found a creature that should not have survived. All these mysteries need to be explained before letting the world know. Saving the children will be the only thing we need to say right now. The rest can come out later. You will be regarded as a hero. I mean we could not have found them if it was not for you and the dogs, and it was you who rescued us from the *Mahaha*."

"I only care about my family and the dog team, nothing else matters to me."

"Well, let's see if we can get you reunited." Sam pulled out his phone and started making calls.

Yuka went to her sled and began making a bed to lay Kikitu on and make him more comfortable.

"Everyone is on their way down," Sam stated after he came off the phone. "It will take them a while as they will mostly slide down on their butts, even the dogs."

She smiled at the thought of seeing her mom and dad, also the dogs, and even the children.

"Can you help me place Kiki on the sled, please?" she asked.

They pulled the sled right up to the dog and together they lifted him onto the bed she had made. Sam took the heavier front with Yuka gently placing the rear legs in a straight position that the elves had suggested.

"If you can wait here," he said, "I will go help some of them down, okay?"

"Sure," she replied.

"If you see a helicopter, wave them down near you."

Yuka nodded as he jumped on the snowmobile and took off up the steep slope, but at least it was a smooth slope made by the avalanche.

The purr of the snow machine slowly died away as it went higher and higher till all was quiet again. She settled down to wait for everyone to come down.

Anticipation of the reunion grew within her. Two long years she had searched for her parents, asking everywhere she went, if anyone had seen or heard of them. Nothing, and now she knew the reason why. They had been snatched by a being that was supposed to have died out.

Out of the corner of her eye a movement attracted her attention. She saw nothing so settled down again, till a rise in the snow level proved she had seen something.

Her heartbeat rose and started to beat fast as a mound of snow slowly rose then a hand broke through. She jumped up, startled, not believing what she was seeing.

She gasped in horror as the arm rose higher. The *Mahaha* was alive and breaking through the snow. Bit by bit, more of the creature appeared. Without thinking, she grabbed the tug line of the sled and began pulling it away, desperately searching for somewhere to hide.

There were no trees, no rocks to conceal them, only a dip at the edge of the avalanche track to sink into. She reached it and dropped down into the slight depression, scooping as much snow as possible in front to hide the sled then fell down beside it looking back towards the animal.

Its head was now free and rising up, shaking snow off at the same time. Then its shoulders appeared and it began shaking the snow off its arms.

Yuka pulled out the sat phone and dialled, waiting. All she got was a busy signal.

"Now what?" she muttered in frustration.

She quickly dialed the other number she had for the officers. It rang and rang and rang.

"Answer! Hurry! *Answer!*" she said in a quiet scream.

"Hello?" Tim finally answered.

"It's not dead." Yuka whispered into the phone.

"Who? What, your sled? You should have it by now," Tim answered.

"No, the *Mahaha* is still alive," she said in a louder voice. "The dart drug must have worn off. It is still alive!" Frustration made her voice get even louder as she tried to tell the RCMP officer.

The creature's head turned towards her as it rose up on two legs. Yuka sank lower into the ground in an effort to hide.

"Do not come down. The animal is up and walking." She watched as it turned. "And it's coming towards me." Yuka switched off the phone, put it back in her pocket, got up and started running.

She knew it was the wrong thing to do, animals always take after running prey, but she wanted to lead it away from Kikitu in the sled.

Never a great runner, she took off downhill as the fastest way out of there. Thudding noises in the ground let her know it was after her. There was no need to turn around and look.

Perhaps if there was a drop off, she could roll away, but there wasn't.

Her heart was pounding, legs heavy trying to run in the snow, then a noise hit her, low and humming.

It made her slow down. It whispered to her.

Her eyes went heavy, sleep beckoned, soft and gentle like a warm sleeping bag.

Then she blacked out.

CHAPTER NINE

"Hold up!" Tim shouted as he stopped the snowmobile, the sat phone still in his hand.

Everyone turned towards his voice, then stopped, or tried to, as some were slip-sliding down the steep slope. The snowmobile engine stopped as he tried to get his voice heard.

"Yuka says the *Mahaha* is alive and breaking out of the snow. The drugs must have worn off. It was only buried in shallow snow so it must have been able to breathe, same as Kikitu, as Sam suggested."

Sam came running up followed by Sakami, Yuka's mother, then Tekke, her father, came sliding across to the snowmobile.

"What did she say?" Sam asked urgently. They all looked concerned.

"That the creature was rising up and walking. She says not to come down. I think she is hiding." He never said it was coming for her, not in front of her mother and father.

"Have we anymore darts?" Sam asked as both the RCMP officers searched the snow machine. They lifted the lids on each compartment.

"None," Tim muttered.

"But we have rifles, right? And bullets, right?" Sam declared. "The two of us must go down and get her back."

"We're coming too," Tekke stated.

"No," Tim asserted. "Too dangerous, you know that, look after the others and wait here till we get back."

Sam jumped onto the rear seat of the snowmobile, it fired up and they shot off downhill, zigzagging as little as possible. Sam pulled out a regular rifle and made sure it was loaded and also that they had more ammunition.

As they got onto the avalanche slope there was no sign of either Yuka, the *Mahaha* or the sled holding Kikitu. They reached the spot that Sam was sure he left them, but the only evidence was a depression in the ground where the creature had risen up.

"Wow!" Tim said. "That is one big animal. I never really got a good look at it before. I must have been in a trance or something."

Sam ignored him as he scanned the surroundings looking for clues. "Over there." He pointed and they drove over to the hump of snow hiding the sled.

Jumping off the machine they examined Kikitu and the sled.

"He's out cold," Tim stated. "Breathing seems normal and pulse as well, but what do I know? I'm not a vet."

Sam looked skyward as they both heard the pulsing beat of helicopter blades. He pulled out his radio and called them to their location.

Swirling snow pounded them as they sheltered their heads with their arms. The rotor blades slowed down when it landed and both officers went to a door that was sliding open.

"It has awakened and took off with our guide," Sam shouted to a group of scientists eagerly looking at him.

"What do you want us to do?" the pilot shouted from up front.

"Hold on a second," Sam replied then turned to Tim. "I think one of us should go search for Yuka in the helicopter while the other gets the rest of the group down here."

Tim nodded in agreement, then Sam turned to the group inside. "Could one or two of you wait here till we get back?"

Nobody seemed willing to get out.

"You and you." He indicated a man and a woman. "Please wait here."

Reluctantly they got out. "Have one or both wait with the sled." Sam told the other officer before getting in.

He checked the rifle was loaded before closing the door, then the group outside stepped away as the rotor blades speeded up and it lifted off the ground.

Gaining altitude, it sped off down the valley, with everyone inside searching the surroundings for any sign of the *Mahaha*. They did not know what they were looking for only that it was tall, white, hairy, walked upright and had stolen another girl.

The white on white was the same as black on black making it hard to tell the difference between mountain and animal on a first pass. They did not notice or observe anything out of the ordinary. The snowy slopes and outlines, shapes and forms were all white and all looked normal.

They turned around after fifteen minutes, went a little higher, and level with the mountain tops, the survey continued.

"You got heat signature sensors?" Sam asked the pilot. "That could pinpoint a creature."

"No, this is only a transport helicopter. Used to move people and equipment around," he answered.

Still nothing, they criss-crossed the valley making sure they covered the whole gorge and surroundings, eventually getting back to where they started.

The snowmobile, adults, children and dogs were just arriving so Sam signalled the pilot to land nearby. Softly it touched down and the engine wound down to a stop.

Sliding the side door open everyone gathered around, inside and out.

"Have you got her?" Yuka's mother asked anxiously, peering inside.

"No, sorry," Sam said. "There was no sign of them. They could not have gone far. It was less than an hour ago since we got the call."

"It was more than that," Tim replied. "But it was only a short time. You're right. They could not have gone that far."

"You don't know the *Mahaha*." Tekke spoke up from the gathering. "We have seen them move fast across the land. They have long legs and big feet that stop them from sinking in the snow."

"Them? What do you mean, them?" a scientist asked. "Is there more than one?"

"Well, we have only seen one at a time but I am sure there is more than one because a different one appeared sometimes," Sakami said.

The pilot appeared from upfront, a tall black man dressed in uniform, headset strung around his neck. "What do you want to do? I don't have enough fuel to fly around all day."

There was silence as they decided on their next move.

"Right now," Sam spoke up. "I think the children are our priority, and we need to get them back home. Have you got a stretcher on board?"

"Yes," someone answered.

"Then I suggest we get all the children and the injured dog back. Then, if you fuel up, we can continue the search. Do you want to unload your gear here and set up a camp?"

100

It seemed there were no objections and the scientists got out and began unloading equipment. Tekke and Sakami took the dogs over to the sled and began hooking them up.

"The dogs will find her," he said quietly. "Why don't you go back with the others?"

"I am not going back without my daughter," she replied. "She has been searching for us since that

Mahaha took us to look after the children so I will not rest till we have her back."

Tim along with Sam appeared with a stretcher and they carefully eased Kikitu onto it then loaded it onboard along with all eight children. The co-pilot made sure they were all secure and belted down.

"There is a veterinary hospital in Silverton," Sam told the co-pilot and the woman nodded.

The whole group that were left turned their backs on the swirling snow kicked up by the rotor blades as the helicopter rose up, turned south, and flew away.

CHAPTER TEN

Yuka awoke to darkness, pitch black without a trace of any light. She waited a moment or two for her eyes to get accustomed but still very little of her surroundings were visible. She stood up, stretched out her arms and walked forward till a solid cave wall confronted her. She turned her head left to right searching for a way out, or a dim light or something to give her a clue what to do next.

A noise grabbed her attention coming from her left. What made that noise? Was it danger or a way out? She stood for a second or two trying to decide and realized she had to do something so she inched her way along the rocky wall towards the sound.

Her foot hit something that clacked and clicked. She bent down to touch what it was and grasped bones, long thin bones that felt like animal leg bones, probably caribou. She let go then stood up to begin moving along further, this time shuffling her feet and feeling for any more obstructions.

At last, she reached a sharp corner and with her heart beating loudly eased her head around to look. A dim glow at the far end of a tunnel shed light on a scene that make her heart beat faster.

Two smaller *Mahaha* figures stood facing each other. Smaller than the first one she had seen, they had to be child *Mahaha's*, barely much bigger than herself. *Must be a family of them*, Yuka thought.

They were making a noise, same as she heard before, and she strained to listen. There were giggling, tittering noises, chuckling and chortling to one another. Fascinated, she stood eavesdropping every whisper and then she realized they were talking to one another, not in any language she had ever heard, in fact it sounded like nothing she had ever heard before.

She put her hand in a pocket and pulled out her sat phone. Perhaps Santa could understand them but the display said no signal. Then, as she went to put the phone back, she dropped it, making a clattering noise. Annoyed she bent down picked it up and put it away.

Too late, the noise had been heard and the two creatures were walking towards her. She turned her head the other way seeking somewhere to run to, but it was just darkness. Fight or flight, she never ran away so she walked out to face them, which made them stop in their tracks.

Chortling noises came out of their mouths, sniggering and giggling away as if trying to confront her, first one then the other kept it up but the tone was the same as if asking questions.

Through sheer panic or backed into a corner sometimes you just grasp at straws and out of her mouth she began giggling also, sniggering that turned to laughter, chuckling that made her chest heave up and down.

Dumbstruck, the *Mahaha's* stared at her in amazement their eyes open wide then crinkled up as if laughing along with her. Yuka tried to communicate. She pressed her hand up and down against her chest then in-between the giggles said, "Me, Yuka."

The creatures said nothing just looked at her curiously. Yuka said it again and uttered her name at the same time. Still no reaction.

The thought of throat singers came to her, wondering if that was the reason why Inuit women tried to make two sounds at once, to try and communicate with the animals.

She tried to copy them, raising her voice to a singing level, calling out her name in between the giggling, laughing, and chirping.

One of them seemed to understand and returned Yuka's song with one of their own. At the end it touched its chest. "Sweeshe," it announced.

The other understood from its sibling and sang the same song then uttered the word, "Sweeshoo."

Yuka started to get excited and began pointing, first one "Sweeshe" then the other, "Sweeshoo" then herself "Yuka." It seemed to get them all excited, and they began pointing at one another calling out their names.

A thudding noise from the darkness made them all go quiet as an adult *Mahaha* emerged from the darkness. It was so large it had to bend over to stop from hitting its head on the roof.

It began to hum, the noise getting louder then spell-binding. Yuka jammed her fingers into her ears as if making a funny face then blew her mouth out as if holding her breath. She felt in control and was not blacking out.

The young *Mahaha's* started making noises like giggling along with calling her name.

"Yuka, Yuka," they said pointing at her and jumping up and down excitedly.

The humming stopped and the adult bent down to get a closer look at her, its face almost touching hers. Panic rose within her but she controlled it and tried to remain calm.

"Yuka?" Its voice was louder and deeper than the young ones. "Y-U-K-A?"

"Yes," she replied then pointed to herself. "Yuka, yes Yuu . . . Uuu . . . Kaa . . . Ahh."

"Sweeshe," she said pointing at one youngster. "Sweeshoo," she said pointing to the other.

Its gorilla-like face got quite excited then. It smiled and Yuka recognised that smile from when she spied on them giggling and tickling the children back at the ledge.

The giggling came out loud and fast as if it were talking to her but she could not understand a word. She held up her hand for it to stop then pointed out towards the light indicating she wanted to go outside.

After a bit of pointing, sign language and giggling she managed to persuade them to take her outside and into the dim light.

The brightness made her close her eyes and turn away towards the darkness of the cave entrance, then she pulled out her sat phone and dialled, hoping she could somehow get help.

"Ho, ho, hello, Yuka! I can tell by the number display it is you. What is going on?" Santa asked. "Is Kikitu all right?"

"He is okay, I think, but I have been taken by the *Mahaha*," she answered.

"Oh dear, that is not good. How can I help? How did it happen? Where are you?"

"The large one who fell in the avalanche woke up and took me to their cave. It seems there is a family of them. I have found out they speak to one another but I cannot understand them or talk to them. Can you translate? Or speak their language?"

"I can try. Let me hear them."

She held the phone between herself and the *Mahaha*.

"Yuka, giggle, laugh, chortle?" she tried to ask a question.

The large creature made some noises as if answering.

"Well, Santa?" She pulled the phone to her ear.

"Sorry Yuka, I have never heard anything like that. It does not make any sense to me. But hold on, I have an older elf who may understand."

She listened as Santa spoke to Mrs. Clause. "Jessica can you summon Eroan here, please?"

As they waited, she felt a slight dread rising within her, what if she could not find the right words to let her go? Or if the creatures got angry? Her mind went back to the pile of bones inside the tunnel.

Finally, a high-pitched voice answered. "Hello Yuka, Eroan here, can you get them to speak?"

She tried to ask some questions as before and the *Mahaha* made some noises that made no sense to Yuka. She asked the elf, "Well, Eroan?"

"Good news, Yuka, I do understand them. They speak an ancient tongue that was last spoken by elves many, many years ago. It is called *Ainut* and was thought to have come from Asia. I have translated it as a record for history and set it on a computer file along with how to pronounce it. If you give me an email address, I can send it to you."

"I am in a bit of trouble right now and not near a computer. Can you speak to them if I put you on speaker phone? Ask them to let me go?"

"I can try. Hold out the phone so they can hear me."

Yuka pressed the speaker phone button and waited.

CHAPTER ELEVEN

Camping equipment was pulled to the edge of the avalanche drift and the scientists began to build a site for tents, monitor stations, and a large communal tent.

Sitka was anxious to find Yuka, jumping up and down in his harness. He knew that with Kiki gone he was now the lead dog and it was up to him to locate their alpha leader, the Inuit girl.

"We had better get going, the sooner the better," Sam said to the group.

"Sakami will ride in the sled and I will guide them," Tekke stated. "Officers, can you follow in on the snowmobile?"

They nodded and climbed aboard the machine. Tekke called "Hike" and the group took off towards a valley below their location.

Speeding downhill, the group reached the valley floor in quick order and after their flying start the dogs settled into their usual fast pace, anxious to get to Yuka.

"Hope they know where we're going," Tim stated from the back of the snowmobile. "I don't see any tracks in the snow only slight depressions."

"The *Mahaha* have very large feet acting like natural snowshoes so they probably don't make tracks like normal animals or humans. The dogs have not let us down so far and they seem really sure where they want to go. Let's trust to their instincts for now."

"Have you tried her sat phone?" Tim asked.

"No signal," Sam replied.

As they traversed the valley, they found deep snow was slowing down the sled. The dogs were having to make jumps to keep going, so Tekke called a halt and everyone stopped. The dogs lay down for a rest while the humans talked.

"This is no good," Tekke said, "the snow is too deep for the dogs to pull the sled."

"What if we just use one dog?" Sam asked. "Let it go, and we will follow in the snowmobile."

"Could work," he replied. "We sure are not going anywhere fast in this. Sitka is the largest and most able to cope with the deep snow. He will find Yuka if anyone can. We will unhitch the dogs, let them rest, and wait here for you."

Sitka was untethered from the tug line and jumped around, glad to be out of the harness.

"Find Yuka." The other dogs called to him as he took off with the snowmobile hard on his heels.

Her parents searched the surrounding mountains in a desperate attempt to see any sign of movement or trace of their daughter but they turned at last to face each other.

"I'm sure they will find her," Tekke tried to reassure his wife.

"I am not going home without her," Sakami stated. "I feel helpless just standing around here."

"What if I check out a little higher ground? Maybe the snow is not so deep and we can find another way to go in the general direction."

"If you like. I will unhitch the dogs. Let them rest here."

Tekke took off up the slope on one side looking for another path, while she began unhitching the dogs from the tug line.

A short time later he came back. "Nothing up that way, it just gets steeper. I will try the other side." He walked past the sled and up the opposite slope.

"No better up that way either." He informed her as he trudged back down the slope in deep snow.

They stood looking at each other as if answers would come to them when suddenly all the dogs stood up their heads pointing up the valley and their ears pricked forward as if listening, then as a group they took off running up the gorge.

The humans could only stare after them. "Whoa, stop, come back." They called out in unison but the dogs paid no attention and the couple could only watch as they disappeared out of sight.

Sitka struggled through the deep snow. In places it got easier but still he had to jump out of the mire that held him back and forward progress was difficult. The snowmobile slid through with ease but if they stopped then it began to sink and getting going again was a struggle.

"The dog is tiring," Tim called out from the back of the machine.

"I can see that," Sam replied. "But he has a big heart and sheer willpower will keep him going. If he slows to a stop, we will let him rest."

Their pace gradually slowed down as the big dog ran out of energy. Eventually, it got to a point where it was stopping for a moment before jumping out and forward.

"Whoa," Sam called out. Sitka turned to look at them then slumped down in a heap, exhausted.

"I have never seen such deep snow," Sam noted as they watched the snowmobile gradually sink into the soft snow. "We better be careful; it could be a S.I.H. You remember, from training, a snow immersion hazard, where we sink so low, we cannot get out."

"Let's get moving then," Tim suggested. "I'll carry the dog on the back, squeeze him between us. When he is rested, we can let him off and see which direction he takes."

They struggled to get the snowmobile moving again then did a loop to come alongside Sitka. Tim coaxed him onto the seat between himself and Sam. The dog was reluctant and was almost hauled aboard.

Heading off in the general direction they were travelling before it was not long before Sitka became restless then suddenly his ears pricked forward.

He jumped off the snowmobile and ran away.

CHAPTER TWELVE

Twittering noises came from the sat phone in Yuka's hand, the *Mahaha's* jumped back in astonishment, totally bewildered by a voice in the girl's hand. They began backing away in alarm, eyes glued to the box that Yuka held. The adult glanced up at her face then back at the phone, questioning with its eyes.

"Eroan, they are frightened by the sat phone. Can you reassure them it's okay, just to trust us?"

The elf's voice changed into a softer tone, cooing like a dove or pigeon. The creatures settled down a little, their bodies relaxing, then they started coming back closer, fascinated by the sounds they were hearing.

When Eroan stopped speaking, the adult Mahaha began chirping, tweeting and chirruping away sounding like anything from a flock of birds to a host of crickets all making noises at the same time.

Yuka tried to understand what was being said. As the conversation between creature and elf changed back and forth, the mood seemed to become friendly and the young *Mahaha's* gazed from adult to phone, each getting more and more excited.

Finally, the voice changed back to English.

"Yuka, I think I have gotten the story from them. Seems that after the Great Beast Wars ended, years ago, a few *Mahaha's* retreated to hide in the mountains. There, they kept out of sight and managed to survive. But now they are dying out. It sounds like they have been infected by a disease, a virus or sickness of some sort and now need help because they do not know how to cure themselves.

"In an effort to communicate with humans, and get help, they stole some children and tried to teach them to speak their language. The nearest noise to them is the giggling sound from the kids. That's why they tickle them, trying to get them to speak in their voice."

"Did they manage to get any of the children to speak to them?" Yuka asked.

"Only odd words but neither understood each other, even your mother and father could not understand them. Very frustrating all around, but I think I have their attention now."

"Will they let me go now?"

"I think we need to sort out their problems first and get communication going between them and the scientists who want to study them."

"What do you suggest?" Yuka enquired.

"Somehow, I have to get the computer file on their language to the scientists so they can work out a way of helping them," Eroan stated.

"If you send it to me, I can get Grandfather or one of my cousins to forward it on to the group of people who are here to find and study them. I just need to get an email address for one of the scientists."

"Give me your email address, and I will send it to you."

"Yuka@Isachuk.com," she answered. "I can phone one of the RCMP and get an email address for a scientist from them."

"Good," Eroan said. "Now how is the battery on your sat phone?"

She looked at the battery indicator. "I am at half charged at the moment . . . 50 per cent."

"Let me explain to the *Mahaha* what is going to happen."

Yuka held out the phone again and a twittering, chirping conversation started between them both. It seemed to last a long time and near the end the adult creature turned its head towards the valley below.

"Yuka, the *Mahaha* says some people are coming towards you. Please be careful and stop any conflict," Eroan said.

When she heard that, Yuka pulled out her dog whistle and blew hard on it to summon the dogs to her, but the *Mahaha's* grabbed their ears and fell to the ground, stung by the whistle's high-pitched blast.

"Eroan, my whistle is distressing the creatures! They have fallen down holding their ears."

"Oh dear, let me reassure them you meant no harm."

Once again, she held out the phone and listened to the conversation, the *Mahaha's* visibly calmed down and stood up. They were wary of her now and kept a distance while occasionally staring down towards the valley.

"Yuka, they are getting worried about what is coming towards them," Eroan said. "You are going to have to intervene and stop or hold back any conflict between humans and *Mahaha*."

"How do I do that?" she asked.

"Put yourself in the middle and hold them away from one another till we can get talking on both sides. I am going to end this call and send you the computer file. I suggest you call the RCMP and explain to them that they have to hold back for now."

"Can you just ask them one more question?"

"What is that?" the Elf replied.

"Ask them what food they have? They seem very thin and hungry, and I don't like the way the big one keeps looking at me as if I was dinner."

Eroan laughed, "Okay, hold out the phone again."

The twittering, chirping continued back and forth before breaking back to English.

"They have not eaten in days. No animals have passed through the valley."

"Well, tell them I will try and get them some food if they will trust me."

After some more twittering the phone went silent. Yuka tried dialing the RCMP.

Sam stopped the Ski-doo and pulled out the ringing phone, "Hello?"

"Sam, this is Yuka. Please stop a minute. Are you on the way up to me?"

"Yes, I am sure Sitka knows where you are. He heard something and took off. Now we are just following his tracks."

"Let me explain something before my battery runs out."

"Go ahead," Sam answered as he turned off the engine of the snowmobile.

"I have managed to communicate with the *Mahaha*," she started. "Don't ask me how, I will explain later. I need an email address for someone in the scientific group so I can send a language file on *Ainut*, which is the language they use. I got it from a friend who studies ancient tongues. I also need you to get them to supply some food. They are starving and need help. Greens as well as meat would be good."

The RCMP officer was astounded. "Yuka, how did you do all this?"

"Sam, I do not have the time. Please get that to them and phone me back with the information."

"Copy that," he replied. "By the way, Sitka should be coming to you."

"Right, goodbye." She cut off the call.

Yuka was not sure how to communicate with the creatures without Eroan but she held out a hand with a thumbs up and a smile.

They gave her a quizzical look but seemed relaxed about the situation, smiles all around till they turned to see Sitka bounding towards them.

The creatures stood upright in an aggressive stance and Yuka jumped between them holding her hands up to calm them and called the dog to her.

Sitka bounded all around her, jumping up and licking her face, so happy to have found her. She petted him, calmed him down then spoke, "Down boy, down."

Exhausted, the dog happily obeyed and lay down on the ground at the same time taking mouthfuls of snow.

"Sweeshe, Sweeshoo," She called them over while patting the dog. "Come meet Sitka." Yuka put her hand on each in turn. "Yuka," she took her hand from her chest and placed it on the dog's head, "Sitka" then pointed to the Mahaha children in turn. "Sweeshe and Sweeshoo."

Gingerly they touched the dog then slowly petted him.

CHAPTER THIRTEEN

Silverton Airport could not really be called an airport. It was only a strip of flat land that had been cleared of bushes, trees, and boulders. It was just long enough to allow bush pilots to land their small planes and long enough for them to take off again. They transported goods, people, or emergency patients to and from cities further south.

At one end was a Quonset hut, a large barn-type structure that could hold a plane and had a room that doubled as a communications hub with radio transceivers, radar, and a weather station.

Outside, a helicopter stood with its doors open as supplies were being loaded. A number of scientists stood around looking skyward as they waited for a plane. In charge was a Professor Robb Cassell.

"Who is this translator we are waiting on?" he asked

"Her name is Dr. Sura Wells from Kimmirut, an expert in ancient and Arctic languages. She speaks Inuktitut, English and another few Native American tongues. She's the only one who has even heard of *Ainut*," a researcher answered.

Shortly after, a small Cessna landed and taxied up to the building and a few people disembarked. A tall woman in a traditional parka carrying a briefcase strode up to the group.

"Hi, I am looking for Professor Cassell, I think," she enquired, her bright blue eyes staring around.

"That's me," he held out his hand and shook hers. They were about the same height, close to six feet, his dark hair and beard contrasted to her pale skin. Both had bright white smiles.

"You have a language file for me?" Sura asked.

"Yes, it's inside if you want to follow me."

As a group they entered the communications room. He showed her to a laptop sitting on a table. She sat down and opened up the file.

"It came from an Inuit girl who stated she has a friend who studies ancient languages," the professor said looking over her shoulder at the screen. "You study those too?"

Without looking up from the screen she replied, "I am collecting them before they are lost altogether. At the moment I am studying the *Tuniit* and *Thule*, Arctic cultures that go back thousands of years. I am surprised anyone knows of the *Ainut* language at all. I have tried to speak it but don't know if I am speaking it correctly."

She hit a button on common phrases and twittering started coming from the speakers. Her eyes opened wide at the verses.

"Wow, if that is correct then I am close but not quite right. I really need to speak with these people."

"They are not people," Robb stated. "It is a long thought to be extinct creature called *Mahaha* found to be still alive in the mountains."

"What?" she exclaimed. "That's impossible. I know their stories but surely they cannot have survived this long without detection."

"Well, that is what we are going to find out. We need you to talk to them," he answered.

She closed up the laptop. "I can't wait to see this, them or whatever is out there."

"Then let's go," he replied. "They are being sheltered or protected by a young Inuit girl called Yuka, who found them. She was taken, but managed to get their trust somehow."

"Not Yuka the sled dog racer is it? She was in the news not long ago. She won the three tribes' race."

"Could be, we don't know but I suggest we go find out."

They all made their way to the helicopter.

The pilot and co-pilot, a black man and white woman, made sure everything was secure, that the passengers were all strapped in, then they went through the take-off procedures. After ten minutes the helicopter took off, swung north and rose up into the sky.

Wearily, Tekke and Sakami had trudged up the mountainside following the tracks in the snow as well as those of the snowmobile. They had left the sled behind after waiting an hour but no one, or dog, had returned.

As they reached a small plateau, a flat tableland, the RCMP were waiting for them as they approached.

"What's going on?" Sakami asked.

"We're not sure, but the dogs have all run up to a *Mahaha* cavern just a little higher. The good news is that Yuka is there."

"She is alive then?" Tekke asked with relief on both parents' faces.

"Yes, but she shouted for us to hang back, to stay away till she sorted things out. That help was coming," Sam answered.

"What sort of help?" her mother enquired.

"Don't know." Sam pulled out his sat phone. "I have been trying to call her but it keeps ringing engaged. Now you're here, I'll try again."

He dialed then listened as the phone rang out and then was answered.

"Yuka, you okay? Your mother and father are here."

"The battery is nearly dead, but put the speaker phone on," she replied.

Sam pressed the button and held out the phone for everyone to listen.

"Mom, Dad you okay?"

"Yes!" they both answered together. "What is happening? You hurt?"

"I'm all right. If the phone cuts out then the battery has run out. Listen, I found out the *Mahaha* speak an old language and have been trying to communicate with humans as they are sick and dying. They need our help to survive.

"I have arranged for a translator and food to be brought here as well as a scientific team. There is a helicopter on its way so watch out for that and guide them down, Sam."

"Copy that," he answered.

"They are very worried and scared so when help arrives send up only the translator and science team leader. I have their trust for now and hope I can come down after they get together."

"You got all the dogs there?" Tekke asked.

"Yes, they are making friends with the *Mahaha* children."

"They have children? How many are there?" Tim asked.

"Two and I think there may be another adult inside the cavern because the big one out here keeps looking inside. I'm sure it wants to go check on whatever is in there."

"How did you manage to gain their trust?" Sam questioned.

"By imitating the voices of the young ones. I don't know what they are saying, but I got their names, which are Sweeshoo and Sweeshe."

"I hear the sound of a helicopter coming," Sam said. "We hope to see you soon."

They broke contact.

CHAPTER FOURTEEN

Plumes of snow pummelled the group as the helicopter touched down and then the whirling blades slowed to a stop giving relief to those on the ground. Soon after, a side door slid opened and people started disembarking, Robb Cassell and Sura Wells approached the group and made introductions.

"We saw the cavern entrance just above as we were landing and a girl in the entrance but no one else," Professor Cassell stated. "Are they hiding inside?"

"You know as much as we do," Sam replied. "Yuka asked us not to go up as the *Mahaha* are very nervous and scared."

"We should go up there right now," Sura said.

"I agree, let's do that, just the two of us."

"You want a gun?" Tim asked as he pulled out his revolver.

"No, definitely not," Robb replied.

They started trudging up the slope when Sura stopped and turned around. "Give us a carton of energy drinks as an offering," she asked and walked back down to the helicopter.

One of the staff pulled out a box and handed it to her then she turned back to continue up the slope.

Yuka stood in the cave entrance watching as the two figures slowly made their way towards her.

"Hi, I'm Yuka," she said as they got together.

"Robb," the professor replied holding out his hand.

"And I am Sura." The woman shook hands with her as well. "Where are they?"

"Just inside. I will go and coax the big one out," Yuka replied. "I don't know its name only the young ones, and they are playing with my dog team."

Inside, she approached the large creature and stretched up to put her hand in its large mitt then pulled it towards the entrance. Slowly they emerged, as the large *Mahaha* stared around timidly.

141

Sura began making noises to introduce herself, chirping, tweeting and singing in a high tone and in the middle said "Sura" with a hand to her chest.

The adult looked at her puzzled, turning its head side to side but the young ones emerged to speak.

"Sura . . . Sweeshoo," it said putting a hand to its chest.

"Sura . . . Sweeshe," the other copied.

"I don't think I am speaking correctly," Sura said to Yuka. "But I am close because the young ones understand."

Yuka could only encourage her with a smile. "Keep trying."

The big creature bent down to look at the woman straight in the face and she backed away warily.

142

"Sss . . . Uuu . . . Rrr . . . Aah," it said slowly slurring the R.

She smiled in return and began speaking again with a trill then a warble putting in a few chirps and squawks. It seemed she got it right because they started talking to each other and while the young ones got excited Yuka could only watch and try to get some sense of what they were saying.

Meantime, the professor opened a box and pulled out a couple of bottled energy drinks. He opened two and handed them to the young *Mahaha* children.

Sura explained what they were and introduced the professor at the same time.

Cautiously, the youngsters sipped from the bottles, then tasting chocolate flavour for the very first time their faces broke into smiles. They gulped the whole lot down and wanted more.

143

Robb opened another couple and handed them round before offering one to the large creature. It seemed like a tiny amount for such a large being but it tipped it down into its mouth.

It also began to smile, a little, then was handed another. That too was swallowed down.

While this was happening Sura was explaining, as best she could, that they were here to help them, to get to know them and tell them about the world outside their territory.

She turned to Yuka and the professor. "Its name is Barma, he just told me and there is another, back there," indicating the cavern, "called Almas. I think it is his mate or companion, not sure of their relationship, but Almas is sick."

"We should go help her," Yuka stated as she grabbed a couple of drinks. "Barma, take Yuka to Almas . . . Almas." She held up the bottles and pointed towards the back of the cave.

"You sure have a way of getting your point over," Sura commented. "No wonder you got to know them."

"When you are desperate you find a way," she replied.

Turning to the creature, they spoke a little before Barma turned and began walking back inside the cave. The rest of them followed behind.

They turned a couple of corners in the dark before reaching another cavern entrance that flooded the room with light. In a corner lay a *Mahaha* stretched out on a bed of animal skins, its eyes opened wide in fear at the sight of the group of figures and looked for answers from Barma.

He reassured her with a soothing voice, telling a story that Sura listened to in fascination.

"What are they saying?" the professor asked.

"He says that at last he has been able to communicate with humans, and we are willing to help. If we let them get to know us, they will get food and maybe we will help the others," Sura said.

"Others?" Robb gasped. "Others? How many are there?"

Sura asked the question, then after the creature replied she turned to them.

"He does not know the idea of numbers, just says not many and some are sick."

"We have got to help them," Yuka stated and walked towards the bed with the bottles of energy drink, opened one and approached Almas.

The creature withdrew its head but Barma spoke softly, urging her to accept Yuka, who held the drink to its mouth and carefully tipped it into her.

It seemed to help as her body relaxed a little. Yuka opened the other bottle and offered it to Almas's mouth. This time she accepted it readily.

"We need to get Oki up here," Yuka stated, turning to the humans.

"Why?" Robb asked.

"I see some blood in her mouth and the teeth look dark. She also has what look like sores or blood at her elbow."

"Who is Oki?" Sura asked.

"Local vet in Silverton," Robb told her then turned to Yuka. "You think that's necessary?"

"Pretty sure. I know I want to be a vet but I am not. It needs medical attention, which is obvious. Do you have a doctor here?"

147

"No, but I could summon one. The nearest one would be further south so may be Oki would be the best bet."

"Can I go ask him? He is looking after my lead dog, Kikitu."

"Let's see what the helicopter pilot says, if the weather is okay and if he has enough fuel."

Sura spoke to Barma explaining they were going to get more help and more food.

The group made their way back to the other entrance, Yuka summoned the dog team to her then, leaving the *Mahaha* behind, made their way down to the helicopter.

Robb and the pilot had a conversation while Yuka hugged her parents. It had been so long since they last saw each other that it was a little strange. When they last saw their little girl, she was their baby but now she seemed like a grown woman even though she was not even a teenager yet. "You have grown up so fast," her mother said with a few tears in her eye.

"I "I had to cope without you and I am not that big," Yuka said with a laugh.

CHAPTER FIFTEEN

Flying was a new experience for her, except for when she was tossed from her sled during a race, and Yuka was fascinated, staring all around at the scenery from the helicopter window. What seemed like long distances on the ground now were only points of view that could be easily reached within minutes not hours of travel.

It was giving her second thoughts. Maybe she would like to be a helicopter pilot instead of a vet or could she do both? The thought of doing both excited her with a new challenge of travelling all over, treating animals and helping people. But then she would have to give up the dogs. That made her think again.

It seemed like no time at all till they were descending into Silverton Airport. Landing near the only building, she noticed that a truck was parked close by.

When she emerged from the helicopter, she was approached by one of the airport staff.

"Hi, I'm Ken. I'll take you to the animal hospital. Oki is expecting you."

150 They jumped in the truck and took off, heading towards the town. The animal rescue station was close by, and they entered by a driveway. The main building was surrounded by kennels and cages to house the animals. Loud barking greeted them as they jumped out of the truck.

Upon entering the building, Oki was standing there with a receptionist. His hair seemed thinner than when she last saw him.

His brown weather-beaten face cracked into a smile. "Nice to see you again!"

"You too," she replied. He never offered to shake her hand so she just smiled back.

"This is Ticasuk, a student working here. She has been looking after Kiki so let's take a look."

They followed the young woman down a corridor lined with lodging rooms for animals. About half-way down she stopped by a wire cage door and opened it.

Kikitu was lying on a straw bed and his tail began wagging, thumping against the floor when Yuka appeared. She ran to him and he lifted his head and licked her face all over but did not try to get up.

"Oh, Kiki, you tried to save me again and it has nearly killed you." She petted and made a fuss of him, a tear in her eye. "How is he doing?"

"He is eating well, gaining strength but we have him sedated a lot. Without him being drugged he would be getting up and hurting himself. He is so strong-willed that he does not understand the need for rest to allow for healing. We need to talk to you about him," Oki said.

"Whatever he needs, I will pay for it," Yuka stated. "I have the money to pay, but not on me, my grandfather has it in trust for me but I can get it." She looked worried.

"It's not the money. I need to talk to you about what happened to him."

"Can we talk later? I need you to come with me to treat a creature in distress," Yuka urged.

"A creature? What sort of creature?" Oki asked, a quizzical look on his face.

"I mean a large animal. I cannot tell you a lot about it, I just need you to come with me and examine it."

"What's the matter with it?" Oki was intrigued.

"I want to be a vet when I grow up so I know a little. I pay attention in school when we do biology as well as ecology, but this animal I think is suffering from malnutrition. It has bleeding from its gums, black teeth and blood spots on its body. We did a nutrition class at school and they talked about sailors who suffered from a bad diet and had what was called scurvy."

"And you think this is what is the matter with this animal?"

"I don't know but I do know it is weak, in distress and needs our help. Will you come with me? I will pay you," Yuka begged him.

"We are quiet at the moment so yes I will come with you. I just need to pick up my medical bag. Ticasuk will take care of your dog but we *will* talk more about him later."

Relieved, Yuka gave him a last petting before leaving. She followed them back to reception and waited while Oki got his supplies.

Together they got back in the truck and sped back to the airport.

The copter blades were beginning to turn so Oki and Yuka jumped on board, they settled into their seats, strapped in and put on headphones with mics so they could talk to one another.

Once in the air Oki turned to Yuka. "Okay, tell me about this animal you are so keen for me to examine."

She hesitated, looking him in the eye before speaking. "You know the stories about the Great Beast Wars, right?"

He nodded. "Well, I found out that the *Mahaha's* did not go extinct."

"*What?*" Oki exclaimed. "You're telling me some are still alive?"

"Yes, the dogs and I found them. They followed its scent after kidnapping children. They were trying to teach them their language so that they could get help from us. After staying hidden for all those years their numbers started going down. They need our help to survive."

Oki stared at her in disbelief. "I don't know if I believe you or not but with all the help you are getting," he looked around the helicopter, "there must be some truth to it. I guess I am going to find out."

"You will see," Yuka replied.

They were quiet for the rest of the journey. Oki kept looking at her. He was about to ask a question then was quiet again. Finally, he spoke. "How big are they?"

"I think they are very thin, that's the way they look to me, but they are very tall with long white hair and big furry feet. Twice your size I would say."

Oki was about to ask more questions when the helicopter began descending slowly, finally touching down and the rotor blades slowing down.

They got out to be greeted by Robb, Sura, and the police officers. The rest of the crew began unloading the cargo.

"Where are Mom and Dad?" Yuka asked.

"They took the dogs to pick up the sled and take it to base camp where the rest of the researchers are.

They are going to wait for you there before going home," Sam reported."

"Let's get you up there to take a look at the *Mahaha*," Sura said to Oki.

Trudging up the short climb to the cavern entrance they found Barma waiting for them. Oki stopped for a moment staring at the large creature. He could not believe his eyes.

Sura and the large animal began talking, explaining that Oki was a medicine man.

The vet turned to Yuka. "They can talk to each other? How is that possible?"

The young girl looked him in the eyes. "I phoned a friend of mine who studies language and found out they were talking *Ainut* and Sura is a translator of that language, perhaps the only one in the country."

"Unbelievable!" Oki uttered.

"Our good luck I would say," she replied.

Entering the darkness of the cave, the professor and Sura switched on their flashlights to illuminate the way. It was not far and soon they entered the room with Almas. She had both youngsters by her side.

Oki was fascinated to see the young *Mahaha's,* and they introduced themselves.

"Sweeshe," holding its hand to it chest. "Sweeshoo." The other did the same.

Getting the idea, the vet held his hand to his chest. "Oki," he said.

Yuka approached Almas, who was lying down, and gently put her hand in hers. She motioned Oki over.

"Oki," she said quietly and he and Sura came close.

The vet looked into her mouth while the translator explained what he was doing.

After a moment he turned to Yuka. "Good job but not quite enough.

CHAPTER SIXTEEN

Oki motioned to Sura, waving his hand up and down the body. "Can you ask her if she has pain anywhere on her body?"

The translator spoke to her and reply came back. "Yes, she has pain in her stomach."

"Ask her if I can place my hands on her and to tell us if it hurts."

Almas agreed and Oki began examining her with his hands, pressing down gently and feeling for anything unusual, then she winched and grunted at one point.

"There, she says it hurts there," Sura told him.

He felt around the spot some more without undue pressure. "I wish I knew this animal's anatomy," he started. "I don't even know what normal blood pressure or temperature is but there is definitely an abnormal lump here. I would need to open it up and find out what it is. Sura, you better ask both the adults if it is okay for me to put her under and cut her open."

While Sura consulted with them, Yuka spoke with Oki. "I can help you. I can monitor its breathing and pulse while you operate. I've done it before."

"Have you now, when was that?" he asked.

"Not long ago," she replied.

"On a certain dog?" he questioned.

Yuka stumbled to find an answer then Sura came back to them before she could reply.

"They have agreed to do it."

"Right," Oki started. "First we have to establish a set of norms or normal reading for a *Mahaha* so I will have to take readings from Barma, if he will sit down somewhere."

Sura explained again to the big one and he sat down on the ground while the vet opened his bag and took out his stethoscope and began listening to different parts of the chest, then measured his pulse rate by holding its wrist to feel the beats.

"Come here, Yuka, listen and feel the pulse."

She observed the readings and took note of the breathing.

"Okay, what's his pulse rate?"

Yuka looked lost. "Normal?" she replied.

"Thought so. Here is what you do. Look at my watch and count the heartbeats for six seconds, got that?" she nodded. "Now multiply that by ten, to get the pulse rate or beats per minute. Try it."

She listened while counting the beats and watching the clock at the same time. "Nine."

"Okay, add a zero to multiply it by ten." Oki stated.

"Ninety beats per minute," Yuka stated.

"That's the heart rate, okay?"

"Got it," Yuka said proudly. "And her breathing?"

"We will only worry about that if it slows right down and that will be obvious. Now let's get started. Find a sitting position by Alma's head and start taking heart rate readings once every couple of minutes or if you detect a sudden change."

Oki opened his bag and began laying out instruments, scalpels, stitching, bandages and injection hypodermic syringe. Looking through some vials of sedative he selected one, inserted it into the plunger and proceeded to put Almas under.

"I don't know the correct dosage to give her. I have never worked on so big a creature but I have given her enough to put a large bull under."

Slowly, Almas fell asleep. Gradually, her breathing stabilized as she settled into a deep slumber.

Oki nodded to Yuka who nodded back as they agreed they were ready. "Sura, can you give a commentary to the big one as I tell you what is happening? If he sees blood he may get upset, worried, and try to interfere."

"Yes, I can do that, if I don't faint," Sura replied then added, "Only joking."

The vet gave her a sideways glance before turning back and began shaving the hair around the area of the surgery then painting the bald patch with an antiseptic solution.

Pressing a scalpel knife into the skin, blood oozed out as he began cutting around the lump. Before he was all the way around, he pulled the skin layer back and laid the flap across the belly.

"As you can see," Oki began, "the tumour, growth or lump is exposed. I can see it has been blocking a tube or stomach conduit so she has trouble digesting food."

Sura translated the story to Barma who look on anxiously.

"Next, I am going to cut the tube and pull out or extract the inflamed growth before sewing the tube back up again to make it whole without any obstruction."

Yuka watched on in fascination as Oki carefully opened the tube and gently pulled out the growth and placed it in a tray. Sura explained what he was doing.

"Normally, I would only let my assistant watch this but I know this is very personal to the creatures so we are all monitoring this operation for their understanding," Oki stated.

He carefully stitched the tube back into a complete composition before placing the flap of skin back and completing the operation by sewing it into place.

"Yuka, is the pulse and breathing normal?" the vet asked.

"I think so," she replied. "It went higher and the breathing slowed but is returning to a steady rhythm."

"Good," Oki stated as he placed a patch bandage over the operation area and held it in place with a sticky cover.

"Think you can nurse the patient for a couple of days or until the scientists can bring a vet in to replace me?" he asked Yuka. "I have to get back to my patients."

"Of course, I can." She felt proud that he would even ask her to look after the *Mahaha*.

"Right." Oki turned to Professor Cassell. "You need to look after this group by giving them good nutritious food till they become healthier. That is up to the vet or doctor you bring in. I will send in a report when I get the results from the lab on the tumour, but I think it is not dangerous."

"I can arrange that, anything else?" he replied.

"No, that's it for now. I would like to discuss the patient's care with Yuka if you would give us a moment."

Everyone left except for the vet and Yuka.

"I am trusting you with the care of this." Oki looked the patient up and down. "*Mahaha,* this is what I need you to do."

Yuka listened intently.

"Do not let her eat any solid food, only energy drinks, a watery soup, or mushy foods like a mashed-up banana. We do not want any solids damaging the tube we just cleared or tearing the stitches. Next, let her rest. We do not want any exercise putting pressure on the operated area."

Yuka nodded to say she understood.

"Now, once a day check the wound by lifting the patch and cleaning gently around the area. Make sure the stitches are holding and no blood is oozing out. We need to keep the area clean and free of infection. If things do not look good, in any way, I want you to phone me and tell me the concern. I will give you my number, my emergency phone number, okay? It's not to be given out. Hopefully they will get a vet out here quickly."

"I have some secret numbers on my satellite phone already so you need not worry," Yuka replied.

Oki gave her a curious stare before carrying on. "Yuka, you have done great work finding the children, the Mahaha and bringing in help. You have proven you are very resourceful and deserve the chance to work with me but only if you answer two questions."

"What are they?" she asked.

"If I give you some books will you study them and . . ." he hesitated. "You have to pass your exams if you want to be a vet. It is a lot of hard work."

"I can do that!" she answered eagerly.

"Next, I have seen x-rays of the work done on your dog and I can see great work has been done to treat him. Since it could not have been you, who did it?"

Yuka held her breath not knowing what to say or tell him. This was a great chance to study and become a vet, something she really wanted to do. Finally, she made up her mind.

"I will tell you if you answer two questions for me."

"What are they?" Oki answered.

"First, can you be trusted with a secret?"

"I keep the confidentiality of all my patients and customers, so I think that is not relevant,"

"Then, do you believe in magic?"

Oki gave her a strange look. "I don't but after what I have seen lately, I am open to being convinced."

Yuka hesitated. "It began one day near Christmas when something fell out of the sky, not a something but a someone!

CHAPTER SEVENTEEN

CHRISTMAS EVE

Jaekwan drove his truck around the back of his house close to the back door. When Tekke and Sakami heard them pull up they rushed out to greet their daughter. Yuka got out the front door of the truck and hugged her mom and dad. They had not had time to reunite properly at the *Mahaha's* cavern, now they held each other close.

"Kikitu is in the back of the truck. Dad can you help Grandfather take him inside?" Yuka asked. "Oki has allowed him home but I have instructions to look after him. He needs medication before sleep."

Tekke let go and went to the rear of the truck to help Jaekwan. A light canvas stretcher held Kikitu and together they slid him out of the truck and carried him inside the house to lay him down on the kitchen floor. Yuka grabbed some books and medication from the front of the truck before closing all the doors, then mother and daughter walked inside. Sakami held her around the shoulder, unwilling to let her go after all the time spent apart.

She laid the books on the table before removing her parka. "I can't believe we will spend Christmas together at last. The last two years have been a nightmare as I searched for you. I always believed you were still alive."

"We are so proud of you," Sakami began. "We have heard all about your adventures: you helping Santa, racing the dog team, helping injured prospectors, then finding us. We wondered if you could survive on your own never mind helping all those people. How did you manage it?"

"I just did what I could. You always taught me to help others, if possible, so that's what I did. Out in the wilderness here we have to help each other, right? That's what you said," Yuka answered.

Tekke laid some hot drinks he had prepared on the table. "Now tell us what happened after we left you at the *Mahaha's* cavern."

"I looked after Almas, the female *Mahaha* for just over a day till they brought in another vet and a doctor then returned on the helicopter to Silverton. All the children had been returned to their families who were very happy that they had returned alive.

"The RCMP and scientists have asked us not to say anything about the *Mahaha's* at the moment until they get a good idea what they are going to do with them.

I suggested they have a village built in a secluded valley and are taught all about the world as we know it then maybe we can get together. I would like to visit them and get to know Sweeshe and Sweeshoo better."

"But how were you able to speak to them. All the time we were with them nobody could understand what they said or what they wanted with us," her mother asked.

"One of Santa's elves, Eroan, knew their language, and we talked over the satellite phone. Santa had given it to me for helping him. No one is to know, it's our secret, we talk sometimes."

"I guess we have to keep the secret as well then?" Tekke said.

"Well, Grandfather knows but please don't let anyone else know," Yuka replied.

She turned towards him. "Grandfather, how are we doing with the funds?"

"Why?" he asked.

"I will have to pay Oki for Kiki's treatment, and I wondered if there was enough to buy a house for Mom and Dad?"

"What!" her parents exclaimed. "What funds?"

"Enough for that and more. I expect you will need to go to university if you want to be a vet."

Sakami and Tekke looked on wide-eyed as Jaekwan explained he had slowly transferred gold nuggets into a fund in Yuka's name.

Speechless, they could only hug their daughter and cry at the same time.

"I did not steal it or even ask for the gold. The prospectors gave it to me as thanks for helping them."

"Oki has given me books to study on animal husbandry. He says I can work at the hospital on school breaks," Yuka explained. "Also, he showed me how to give Kikitu his pills."

She took a medication tablet from a bottle and leaned down to Kiki's head. His tail started wagging, thumping up and down on the floor.

"You put your hand under his chin, like this, then gently squeeze the sides of his mouth with your thumb on one side and fingers on the other till he opens his mouth."

She looked into the mouth. "Then you pop the pill right down his throat then close it and hold it closed till he swallows."

Kikitu was used to it by now and swallowed. "See?" Yuka smiled. "It's easy."

"Looks like you have a knack for it," Jaekwan commented.

Yuka stood up looking pleased with herself.

"Let's have some supper before you go to bed." Her mother said. "I prepared some stew for us." She laid some bowls on the table and started dishing it out.

They sat eating quietly till Yuka spoke. "Can Kiki sleep in my room tonight? I want to keep a check on him."

"You know he always sleeps outside with the others," Jaekwan replied.

"But he will get excited being close to the rest of the team. Just for one night, please," she pleaded. "I will take him outside tomorrow and get him started on gentle motion and rehab."

The adults looked at one another questioning the request and with nods Tekke spoke. "We guess it will be all right for one night but only tonight . . . right?"

Yuka smiled. "Thanks, he will like sleeping with me. He always stays close to me when on our travels."

"About that," her father started. "You know we will need the sled and dog team to go looking for food again. Your grandfather says he will get a new pup to replace Kikitu, so he will be with you all the time."

179

"I guessed that would happen but can I have the team sometimes to go visit our relatives?"

"I think we can allow that," Tekke looked at her mother for approval and she nodded.

"Great, then I will take Kikitu for walks. He can accompany me to school and wait outside. Everyone knows him and they like to pet him. He's a big softie and loves all the attention."

It went quiet again while they finished supper. Afterwards, the two male adults lifted Kikitu and carried him into Yuka's bedroom laying him gently on the rug beside her bed.

"I'm going to have a shower and wash my hair before going to bed," Yuka said and went around hugging and kissing before saying goodnight.

She kept popping in and out of the bedroom, getting a shower, brushing her teeth, washing her hair, putting on her favourite dog paw PJs then drying her hair. She wafted the hot air from the dryer over Kikitu who snapped his jaws at it, never having felt hot air before. Yuka laughed.

When her hair was dry, she petted Kiki before settling down under the covers. It was Christmas Eve but she was not thinking about presents, just feeling tired but happy to be home with her parents. She soon fell asleep.

CHAPTER EIGHTEEN

THUMP, *thump, thump . . . the noise woke* Yuka up. Without opening her eyes, she stretched one hand out of the covers and placed it on top of the dog.

"What is it, Kiki? I hope you don't want to go outside in the middle of the night."

Gradually she opened her eyes and noticed a strange glow in the room. Soft and golden, it flickered around as if being swayed or moved around. She lifted her head to see what was causing the radiance then her eyes opened wide.

"Santa, what are you doing?"

"Ho, ho, I'm just admiring your sled dog race trophy."

Holding it up before him, a headlamp on his forehead shone directly into the cut glass mountain-shaped award, the dog sled in the middle spilling light off in all directions filling the room with all kinds of shapes and silhouettes.

"Marvellous, marvellous, you did a great job there," he said while placing it back on her dressing table.

"I told you they were the best sled dog team around, but Santa how come I am not asleep? You are supposed to sprinkle dust over the house to keep us all sleeping while you are in here."

"Because I wanted to speak to you." He wandered over to her bedside and knelt down beside Kikitu then spoke to him. "You keep quiet and take it easy. You will get better faster if you move slowly till your injuries heal up."

As he petted him, Kikitu started licking his face. "Ho, ho, ho . . . you are a sloppy one."

Yuka raised herself up on one arm. "But why?"

"I made this my last stop before getting back to the North Pole, or I should say Christmas Island. Everyone calls it the North Pole but there is no land there only ice, but no matter, you know what I mean."

"Yes, but what for?" Yuka asked again.

"To thank you, Yuka. Because of you I had to deliver eight more Christmas presents to four happy families. You brought a lot of joy this Christmas and that is what it is all about.

Spreading hope, happiness and joy helps us move forward to face a new year after a year of uncertainty, not knowing where our children or parents are, not knowing how we are going to survive, all the difficulties we have faced.

"Now we can enjoy this gift of having each other around as well as the giving and receiving of presents."

"I am just happy to get my parents back; don't think I am bothered about presents," Yuka said.

"I know, I know," Santa said. "You are getting older and soon you will be too old for presents from me, once you become a teenager it will stop but just enjoy them anyway. You have done so much good that I could almost make you one of my elves except you are too big."

"I'm not that big," she called out quietly.

"Sorry, but you have other things to do."

"Like what?"

"If you become a vet then you will be helping animals as well as pet owners. You have lots to do so just keep doing what you are doing. We will keep in touch and maybe we can have you to one of our . . . after-Christmas elves tea and cookie parties."

"I would like that," Yuka said with a sigh.

"I have lots of cookies in the sleigh this year all made by children. If I were to eat them all I would be as big as the sleigh outside! Ho . . . Ho . . . Ho! Guess I will have to get going. Jessica will have the kettle on and will make me a nice cup of tea when I get home . . . and, this year I will have lots of stories to tell the elves of *Mahaha's*, RCMP searching for children and you finding them."

He bent down to kiss her on the forehead but because of ice or snow on his beard it was like being kissed by a wet walrus. She fell back on the pillow, wiping her head with her forearm.

"I think you are the sloppy one, Santa, not Kikitu."

"Ho . . . ho, sorry about that," he laughed. "Now I am going to put you back to sleep or you will stay awake for the rest of the night, probably get up and waken all the rest of the family."

Pulling a pinch of dust from his coat pocket he sprinkled it out in the air where it shone like multi-coloured diamonds. Yuka gazed at it with fascination.

"Good night, Yuka."

"Good night, Sa . . . n . . . t . . .a." Her eyes closed.

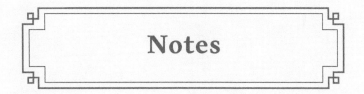

Notes

If you want more information about subjects found in this book, I urge you to do Internet searches using keywords like:

Inuit Cultures, Traditions and History
Lifestyles of the Inuit
Inuit Mythology
Amauti
Suaasat
Aurora or Northern Lights
Komatik sled
Travel Nunavut
Astronomical Twilight

◆ FriesenPress

Suite 300 - 990 Fort St
Victoria, BC, V8V 3K2
Canada

www.friesenpress.com

ISBN
978-1-5255-5405-6 (Hardcover)
978-1-5255-5406-3 (Paperback)
978-1-5255-5407-0 (eBook)

1. JUVENILE FICTION, ANIMALS, DOGS

Distributed to the trade by The Ingram Book Company

CPSIA information can be obtained
at www.ICGtesting.com
Printed in the USA
LVHW070211190320
650510LV00001B/1

9 781525 554063